# The Poet And The Ca[...]

## Peak District Detective J[...]
## Series Two
## Volume One

I would like to thank all my friends and supporting colleagues for their efforts in bringing John Gammon to the second series of five books.

All the John Gammon books are available on Amazon. I have also have two more books on Amazon. One an historical love story tinged with time travel. An intriguing book called "Looking For Shona"

The Poet And The Calling Card

Another book also available is "Got to Keep Running" A young lady on the run from people who will harm her. She finds happiness in the Peak District but will it last?

For all John Gammon readers the first book "Things Will Never Be The Same Again" in the first series is now available on Amazon on audio form.

It was a great experience hearing the characters which you will have read about come to life. A big thank you to Mary Phillips and her company Riveting Narration for an excellent job.

# The Poet And The Calling Card

## C J Galtrey

# The Poet And The Calling Card

This book is a work of fiction. Names, characters, organisation, places, events and incidents are either products of the author's imagination or are used fictitiously.

All rights reserved.

No part of this book maybe reproduced or stored in a retrieval system or transmitted in any form or by any means, electronic, mechanical, photocopying, recording or otherwise without express permission from the author in writing.

C J Galtrey.

# The Poet And The Calling Card

## JOHN GAMMON

The second, in a series, of books about Detective Inspector John Gammon, written by C J Galtrey.

Detective Inspector John Gammon of Bixton Police finds himself in the middle of a set of murders leading up to the Christmas period.

DI John Gammon is about to have a Christmas like no other.

Enjoy this detective mystery set in the beautiful Peak District of Derbyshire.

The book holds lots of twist and turns for John Gammon, happiness, sadness, grief and intrigue.

The beautiful Peak District is yet again the setting for this thriller.

# The Poet And The Calling Card

It was Monday November 2nd 2015. John Gammon stood looking out of his office window towards Losehill the rain lashing down on his office window. He could not believe how beautiful the Peak District still was even in all this bad weather, it still gave out an air of majesty to all who looked upon her.

Gammon stood in a world of his own, his thoughts being pulled towards the fact that Chan Chi was still on the run and DCI Gammon still felt uneasy about the case. Gammon still hadn't found his half-sister in France, which was beginning to bother him.

Suddenly there was a loud knock on his office door which brought John back into reality. "Come in".

Inspector Smarty looked shaken, his face was ashen. "What's the problem Dave?"

# The Poet And The Calling Card

"You need to come Sir, there has been a body found in Pritwich". "It's not your first Dave, why do you look so horrified?" "Sir, the victim's body was found with a piece of wire around her neck, which almost decapitated her. There is something else Sir, whoever did this then placed a business card, which was found in her handbag, with blood on it. It is one of yours Sir?" "What?" said Gammon.

"Forensics are on site now Sir". "Come on Smarty, let's get over there". They travelled in Smarty's car through the dales eventually arriving at the pretty village of Pritwich. Smarty parked outside the village Church. There was a crowd of onlookers already gathered but the Forensic boys had managed to get the tents up to stop the prying eyes.

The rain was pretty heavy as they left the car. "Feels like we are being hit with a fire hose Sir". "Yes not ideal Smarty. Excuse me let me through please". Smarty barged

## The Poet And The Calling Card

his way onto the muddy climb to where the body was being looked at. Head of Forensics John Walvin met Gammon and Smarty outside the tent. "Not a pretty one this lads, this body has been in the ground for a fair few months looking at the rate of discomposure and the wildlife have had nibble too".

"So what've we got Wally?" "Can't be too specific at the moment because of the state of the body, but I would say she is about twenty five to thirty years old, she has a small tattoo on her back of Winnie The Pooh, I'm sure we are all familiar with the character of the books. She has been tortured, so she wasn't killed here I don't think. If you can give me twenty four hours I should be able to give you a whole lot more". "Ok Wally, as soon as you can mate. Come on Smarty, I have seen enough why anyone would want to play about with dead bodies is beyond me" "Know what you mean Sir, it's a bit like

## The Poet And The Calling Card

dentistry who would want to do that for a living?" "When we get back Smarty, let's see if we have any records of a girl with Winnie the Pooh tattoos" "Will do Sir".

They arrived back at Bixton at lunchtime. Gammon returned to his office and carried on with his post, the last letter to be opened was in an orange envelope, the kind you see people sending birthday cards in. Gammon opened the envelope and a razor blade fell out. He thought how unusual as most people had safety razors these days. He carefully undid the letter.

*"Dear Chief Inspector*

*Hope my little letter hasn't ruined your day? Being the nice person I am I have taken the time to write this letter. Now that you have found Winnie the Pooh girl*

# The Poet And The Calling Card

*there will be a total of seven murders in the Peak District all in different circumstances, Some will be buried who, I will keep alive, but only just. I will send you a poem as a clue and if you crack it, then you will save one of these girls. From the date you receive the poem, you will have two weeks to crack it. On the last minute of the final day, the victim will die. Fun game hey Gammon? The razor blade is your clue before I send you the poem, see I am being nice. Goodbye for now I will be in touch"*

**The Poet**

The writers hand writing was very scrawny and Gammon thought he may have been ill educated yet his spelling was good. Gammon felt sick to the pit of his stomach. Sergeant Milton walked past the office. Gammon barked at him. "Get this down to Forensics and I want answers tell them". "Yes Sir" and Milton took the letter and the envelope that Gammon had

## The Poet And The Calling Card

put in an identification bag and set off for Forensics.

"Shit here we go again", Gammon thought. They were already a couple of officers down, with Scooper off with the flu and Bancock touring Australia for six weeks. Gammon rung down to the front desk and informed Sergeant Yap that he wanted everyone in a meeting in the incident room at 9.30am in the morning.

Milton came back to Gammon's office. "They will have the results on the body and the letter by 9.00am in the morning Sir". "Ok thanks, Carl". Milton turned to go and Gammon knew he had been a bit sharp with him. "Do you fancy a pint on the way home at the Tow'd Man Carl? My treat?" "Can do Sir; just let me get my coat. I will follow you up there Sir". "Ok Carl, I'll meet you there".

It was one of those nights where you feel like any sunshine you'd had was years

## The Poet And The Calling Card

ago. It was dark and the rain was still coming down in bucket loads. It was quite a bad drive up to the Tow'd Man and John wasn't sure of the reception he might get from Saron or Angelina come to think of it. Word had got out that he was seeing quite a bit of Inspector Scooper.

Saron and Angelina had spent a lot of money at the pub they had kept the inside almost the same but had built a couple more rooms on the back for meals and above for accommodation.

John walked in under the low beam covering the top of the door with the sign saying "Duck or Grouse" and he had banged his head many times over the past few years. It was only 5.45pm but the bar and eating areas were full. The girls had certainly made a nice job of the pub.

"Hello John what can I get you?" "I'll have a pint of the Pritwich Witch, please Angelina". Quick as a flash Saron

## The Poet And The Calling Card

commented "Thought you would have had enough of the Pritwich Witch with your mate Scooper" John just glanced at her then gave Angelina the money for his beer. Carl arrived and decided on a pint of Stella.

"What was going off in the grounds of Pritwich Church today, John?" "We appear to have found a body Saron, but that's all I can say at this time" and he smiled. She smiled back at him knowing she should not have said anything about the Pritwich Witch.

"Hey John how are you?" "Not bad Bob. Yourself?". "Can't grumble mate. We've just had a four day cruise to Florence, which was, nice just charging the batteries up for the Christmas break". "Where is she tonight?" "Cheryl?" "Well yes, unless you have done a swap" and John laughed. "She's gone to badminton at Pritwich Village Hall with Carol Lestar and Doreen from the Spinning Jenny. I think Sheba

# The Poet And The Calling Card

Filey goes as well. They will be in about 9.00pm, drinking like fish because they think they will have lost weight playing badminton".

"That's a bit cynical there Bob old lad". "You reckon John? Just wait and see. Anyway where have you been hiding not seen you for a few weeks".

"Well I moved down to Mum and Dads farm now that the holiday cottages are done". "So you are living in one of them now then?" "Yeah, so been busy decorating and stuff".

"What the hell happened in Pritwich today, John? I called for a quick one at the Sycamore and spoke with Tony and Rita, they said they have had their busiest lunch time since they took the pub. All the media lads had been in for meals". "There has been a body discovered in the fields adjacent to the Church Bob, can't tell you more than that until it is announced to the

# The Poet And The Calling Card

press officially". "I understand mate. Hey look who's here and just in time seeing that I am in the chair".

"How are we Bob?" "Good thanks Steve, what are you having?" "I'll have the same as my mate", he said nodding at John's pint. "No Jo tonight?" "Her sister is up from London and she is staying with us. Apparently she has split from her husband and is going to be staying with us for a few weeks". "Bloody hell, don't introduce her to Gammon". "And what is that supposed to mean, Pants on Yer Head Bob?" "Well let's be honest you are the ram around here old lad". "Ha ha you are so funny Bob, just get the drinks in".

"So, what's the sister in laws name then Steve?" "Tracey Rodgers. She married Martyn Rodgers from Micklock, he had a good job down in London something to do with Aerospace. I think he was quite high up, so they live in London". "You will have to introduce me Steve". "Steady

# The Poet And The Calling Card

Porky, you have enough on your plate". "Give over, I only meant I would like to meet her. Was she at your wedding?" "No he had to go to Brazil with work and he liked her to go with him. Think he was a bit of a control freak to be honest". "Does she look like Jo?" "Well yeah, sort of, she has quite long blonde hair which covers the most stunning eyes". "Well I best get a meeting then Stevie boy". "Be quiet Bob, the bloody Gob is coming back!!"

"What are you two talking about?" "Daren't tell you Bob, you might put it in your stage act". "That reminds me, did I tell you about the rabbit going into a pub?" "Talk in a bit Bob" and Steve and John left Bob telling his joke to some innocent holiday maker who looked like a rabbit trapped in a car's headlights.

"Now then old lad, how are you? And what about you Mr Lineman?" "I'm good Jack". "Don't ask about me you two, I'm hurt!!" "Sorry Shelley and how are you

# The Poet And The Calling Card

my lovely?" "You're a bloody creep Steve". "Come here John, let me give my favourite copper a kiss". John leaned forward and Shelly planted a kiss on his cheek. "Lovely to see you, where have you been hiding?"

"I've just been telling Steve I have moved into one of the holiday cottages down at Mum's farm. Guess I shouldn't say that anymore now that it's Rogers" "It will always be Phil's and Emily's farm to me John". "Thanks Shelley. Anyway, I have been decorating and getting it just how I want it". "Me and John had a walk past there last week, you have made a lovely job of the cottages. Roger showed us them". "Well thanks Shelley but Jayne Thornley-Coil did the hard work, with Posh Pete. She is brilliant don't you think?". "Me and Jo are going to use her for the barns at the back of the house and the Victorian Orangery". "Your place is

# The Poet And The Calling Card

stunning Steve" "Thanks Shelly, we are pleased with it"

"What's the entertainment tonight Shelley?" "The Mother Pearl Girls, they do soul music and a bit of sixties". "Where are they from?" "Some relation of Doreen and Kev's at the Spinning Jenny I think". "Hi John" "Speak of the devil, it's the badminton girls". "Hope you haven't been saying anything nasty about me John". "No not at all Doreen. Hi Sheba how are you?" Sheba gave John the gypsy minx look and smiled. "Are you not speaking to me?" "Of course Cheryl, how are you? Still suffering Bob's awful jokes and Jackie's cake icing?" and she laughed.

"I hear there has been a body found at Pritwich?" "Yeah, I can't say much yet, although we hope to have it identified by morning".

"Are you dancing John?" "Thought you would never ask Sheba, I love this one

# The Poet And The Calling Card

"Bernadette the Four Tops"". John and Sheba went off to the dance floor. "Didn't take old Porky long to score?" "Only jealous Mr Lineman, I am too!" Shelly and Steve laughed.

"So where's Sandra tonight John?" "She has the flu", he replied. "Are you two living together now then?" "No it's not full blown". I'll bet you say that to all the girls Mr Gammon". "No, seriously we just see each other a bit, that's all". "Gammon you are so full of shit what about poor Saron? Oh and Joni? Plus I don't know how many others. You are having a laugh Mr Gammon". John felt quite embarrassed at Sheba's words and decided to say nothing. After a few seconds silence Sheba burst out laughing "Gotcha" she said. "Blimey thought you meant it Sheba". "Sorry John, I couldn't help myself".

The dance finished and they wandered back to the table. "Fancy a dance with me

# The Poet And The Calling Card

Sheba, you are in demand?" "Not with a married man, I'm not Cheryl thanks Steve, but best not". "It's only a dance". Sheba flicked her hair and took herself off to, powder her nose, as she put it.

John realising Sheba was playing him somewhat, decided to sit with Steve, John and Shelley for the rest of the night. Saron was busy all night so he never got a chance to speak to her, other than to say goodnight. Angelina had been on the bar all day, so she had finished early.

John took a steady drive to his cottage. There were no tourists booked in the other cottages, which was unusual. Every cottage had been taken since the opening day. It felt nice and peaceful as he pulled into the parking spot. His renovated limestone barn glistened in the moonlight the spar acting like small diamonds.

# The Poet And The Calling Card

Roger Glazeback had carried on in the same vain as Philip Gammon. The yard was tidy and always very clean for a farm.

John's cottage had two bedrooms, both with en-suite bathrooms; a large dining kitchen; and a downstairs toilet, far more than John needed. He opened the cottage door and picked up his mail.

The date had been arranged for the handing over of funds to the hospital and the renaming of it to, Annie Tanney Cottage Hospital. 'That just leaves the houses to sort' he thought to himself. John poured a large glass of Jameson's whisky and made his way up to bed.

The alarm went off at 7.30am, John stretched and leaned onto the bedside table for the TV remote. Sky news was the first channel to come on. ISIS had blown up a hospital in Syria, dreadful scenes. The next report to come on made John sit up.

# The Poet And The Calling Card

"Andrew Lord, Sky News, Pritwich Derbyshire. Yesterday a body was found in this sleepy village of Pritwich, alongside the local 15$^{th}$ Century Church. As yet police have not confirmed the name of the victim or how she died, but we have an exclusive interview right now with a local man. Mr Laurence Hall, "Mr Hall can you give our viewers an insight into what you know about this grisly find in your village?" "She was a lass, I know that much" "What sort of age Mr Hall?" "They said about twenty eight". John was fuming what a load of bullshit he didn't even know her age.

"How was she murdered Mr Hall?" "Stab wounds I was told". "Well thank you Mr Hall, this is Andrew Lord from Sky News in Pritwich in the Peak District". John was fuming he quickly showered and left for work. On the way he called a contact he had at Sky News, Jimmy Green.

# The Poet And The Calling Card

"Jimmy? John Gammon here Bixton Police" "Hi John you got a scoop for me?" "No I want a bloody retraction. That guy you just had on made all that up. We don't know the age of the girl and off the record she wasn't stabbed" "A bit of artist license there John, no harm done" "That depends if your daughter is missing and is aged twenty eight, Jimmy that was bloody irresponsible" "Tell you what I will do John, you give us some info and I will retract Hall's interview and apologise". "Get stuffed Jimmy, you are all the bloody same, total parasites". With that John disconnected the call.

"Morning Sir" "Morning Yap, is the meeting set up for this morning?" "Yes Sir". Gammon climbed the stairs and grabbed a coffee out of the drinks machine on his way. Every morning he thought that he should get himself a coffee machine for his office as this coffee was like dish water, but he never did.

# The Poet And The Calling Card

Gammon started on his post. There was nothing sparkling, until he got half way down. There staring at him was another orange envelope. He carefully opened it, inside was a scrawny note. "Hi John, I hope you don't mind me calling you John, but if we are going to have fun playing this game we should be friends" and he had drawn a smiley face. That was it, nothing else, other than that he had signed off "The Poet".

By now it was 9.30am Gammon took the envelope and note down to the incident room. Every officer was there, except Scooper who was still not well, Bancock was on extended leave and Yap was looking after the front desk.

"Right good morning everyone, by now I am sure word has got round we have another nutter on our patch. Wally what have you got for me/" "The victim was approximately thirty one years of age. She was very undernourished when she died.

# The Poet And The Calling Card

She had small marks on her back like somebody scraped her back with a cheese grater in some kind of torturous way. We found no evidence she had been sexually assaulted. Her dental records show her to be a Mandy Nichol". "So what was the razor blade reference about in the orange envelope Wally?" "I don't know Sir, the blood we found was hers. We have no DNA from the killer. The business card with your details is actually one of your own business cards, we found your DNA on it Sir. It looks like somebody who has access to your business cards. Finally Mandy was severely garrotted with very sharp wire, possibly piano wire".

"Ok thanks Wally and thanks to your team for the urgency shown. Before you go Wally, I've had another orange envelope in the post, just run it for prints, DNA etc". "No problem Sir".

"Ok team here we go again. As you know we are a bit short staffed, so I am bringing

## The Poet And The Calling Card

in an officer from Yorkshire until Bancock gets back. He will be here in the morning his name is Warren Cus'tard and no, you don't say his name like Custard as in on your pudding, it's apparently Cus.Tar'd his father was Portuguese but I am sure you lot will have a nickname by the time he gets here!!".

"Right Milton, find out where this girl is from and who her next of kin is? Smarty, check out everyone in the area that sells this colour and size of envelope and when you find the shops I want any CCTV checking. The postmark is Rowksly, however, this could be a decoy but I want to know where the business cards are printed for the station and I also want to know if any cleaners at the station have criminal records. That's anybody that has cleaned at the station in the last year. Come on then get on it".

They all scurried off to do Gammon's bidding. Gammon walked across to his

# The Poet And The Calling Card

desk sergeant. "When do the cleaners come in and more to the point, at what time do they clean my office?" "They usually come on as I am handing over to Sergeant Trimble Sir" "Do I have to guess Sergeant Yap or are you under some assumption I can read your mind?" "Sorry Sir, around 6.15pm". "Is it the same crew every time?" "Can't say for certain because I don't always see them, but the ones I have seen were a man and his wife, I think his name is Lonnie and his wife is Babs and the other guy is Polish or Latvian and I think they call him Rinko" "Ok, thanks Yap".

Gammon climbed the stairs, halfway up he met Milton. "We've got an address for the victim Sir" "Go on then!!" "It's Number 33 Gell Avenue Ackbourne, Sir". "Get your coat Milton we are going to inform the next of kin".

Milton drove to Ackbourne, Gammon was feeling very tetchy. "Rough area this Sir,

## The Poet And The Calling Card

the beat lads always go in two's on this estate". They pulled onto Dovedale Avenue took the next left onto Nestle Road.

On the corner there was a gang of kids stood smoking and drinking cans of cider, all on BMX bikes and aged between ten and fifteen, Gammon thought. As Milton drove past, they all stuck one finger at them, one of the kids threw a can of beer at the car. Milton quickly pulled over but by the time he had stopped, they were fleeing. The language aimed at them was disgusting.

"Little shit's where the bloody hell is their parents and why aren't they at school?" "Leave it Milton, get back in the car, let's get this over and done with and get out of this shit hole". They pulled up outside Number 33 Gell Avenue. The house looked horrendous, any curtains at the windows were hanging half up or were closed. The weeds in the garden engulfed

# The Poet And The Calling Card

what had once been an ice cream van in its day.

"Stay with the vehicle Carl". Gammon set off down the broken tarmac path strewn with cigarette butts. Finally he knocked on the back kitchen door. As he waited he thought the last time this place had been painted Queen Victoria must have been on the throne. Eventually after a lot of vile language coming from inside the house a woman appeared. "What the f**k do you want, we've got enough weed, now piss off".

Gammon pulled out his warrant card. "Are you Mrs Nichol?" "I'm Mrs Lounds now. I was Mrs Nichol until he buggered off with her over'th road about eight years ago" "Can I come in Mrs Lounds?" "Have you got a warrant?" "No I do not, but I really don't want to do this stood on the doorstep" "You'd better come in then, mind the dog shit I ain't had chance to clean it up yet".

# The Poet And The Calling Card

The sink was full of dirty pots and there were Chinese take away cartons everywhere. "Come through". Sat in an armchair was a big guy that Gammon thought he recognised. Gammon showed him his warrant card. He suddenly clicked he was one of Lund's protection guys back in the day.

"What the bleedin' hell do you want?" "I am afraid I have some bad news. Do you have a daughter Mrs Lounds, called Mandy Nichol?" "Yeah, what's she bloody done now, silly bitch?" "I am sorry to tell you, she was found murdered yesterday in Pritwich".

The woman showed no emotion. "Well I'm not bloody surprised, the people she ran with, hey Terry?" Terry Lounds didn't answer he knew Gammon had clocked him. "Is that it then?" "We would like you to identify your daughter's body" "Will you lot bury her? I ain't got any money".

# The Poet And The Calling Card

Gammon was having all on holding his tongue. The place stunk of weed and she says she can't afford to bury her own daughter. "Bloody skank" he thought. "I can't decide that, but I will send a police car to pick you up and if you require a liaison officer to help you through the grief, then that can also be arranged Mrs Lounds". "Tell the copper that comes for us we will meet him outside Lidl at 2.00pm, can't have anyone off this estate see me talking to coppers". With this Gammon had heard enough so he left.

As he approached the car, a kid wearing a hoodie and on a BMX bike, threw a bottle. It just missed Gammon's head but broke the driver's side mirror on the car. Gammon quickly got in. "Go Carl, let's get out of this place".

The ride back to Bixton was quiet, just the odd try at a conversation from Milton. Back at the station Smarty was waiting. "Just let me get Yap to pick up that poor

# The Poet And The Calling Card

girl's mother, she was a hell of a bowl of wax". Gammon gave Yap the instructions and walked back to Smarty. "Milton come with me, let's go to Inspector Smarty's office".

"So what we got Dave? "The cleaning company have been doing the station for some fifteen years. The man and woman have always done it, but the Polish guy Rinko, only started cleaning here four months ago but he has worked for them for sixteen months. I have contacted Polish police and guess what? Our Rinko Bolan, has a record for violence toward women in his native Poland. He has also been done for burglary and theft" "Right, get this bastard in for an interview, how the hell can somebody like that be cleaning a police station?" "I did ask that of the cleaning company, but it appears he had false papers". "I can't believe this country Dave, I really can't. Right, what else?"

# The Poet And The Calling Card

"We have three shops in an area covering Bixton and the outside villagers, only one of the three stocks this envelope and guess where they are supplied from? "Not bloody Poland?" "You got it Sir" "So the shop that sells them, have they sold any to a Polish man, do they know?" "Well this where we come unstuck Sir, the guy that owned the shop had a heart attack and died three month ago. So this guy is the new owner, so he doesn't have much history".

"Damn and we were doing so well. Right bring this guy in at 11.00am tomorrow and let's get a search warrant to search his house. Milton, will you get that sorted now? Also make sure he has a solicitor with him tomorrow" "Right ok Sir". Gammon turned to Smarty. "This could be our quickest solving of a murder ever Dave" "Certainly looks that way Sir". Just then Gammon's phone rang.

"John?" "Hi Sandra, how are you feeling?" "Loads better, I should be back

## The Poet And The Calling Card

in tomorrow. Did you want to pick me up for a drink? Mum's got Rosie overnight" "Yes that would be good, do you want to eat? Fancy the Spinning Jenny? I'll phone Doreen in case she is busy and pick you up straight from work then we can have a drink somewhere else if you want?" "Sounds good to me handsome" "Flattery will get you everywhere Sandra" "See you in a bit"

Gammon climbed the stairs to his office and sat gathering his thoughts. He really could not believe the mother of the poor girl who was murdered and there was no doubt he would be bringing her in for questioning.

"Sir?" Milton stood at Gammon's office door. "Yes Carl" "We've just had Kent police on, Chi Chan was detained at Dover this morning and he is on his way back to Derbyshire, should be here by 4.30pm" "£Great news Carl, looks like we are getting a few breaks for once".

# The Poet And The Calling Card

Milton left; it was almost 4.15pm so hopefully Chan Chi would be here soon. It was about 4.00pm when Milton came back. "What is it Milton?" "Chan Chi has escaped Sir, the two police officers guarding him were found dead at the road side near Ackbourne. It appears they were ambushed" "I don't bloody believe this". The phone rang. "Hello" Gammon retorted in an aggressive manner. "Sir I have the Chief Constable of Kent police on the line for you" "Ok Yap, put him through. Good afternoon Sir" "Nothing good about this situation Chief Inspector Gammon. I am told I have lost two officers because of Derbyshire's Constabulary inept attitude to my officers". Gammon tried to defend himself but Kent Chief Constable, Sir Christopher Pummel, was having none of it. Pummel's parting shot was that he would have Gammon on traffic by the end of the week.

# The Poet And The Calling Card

Gammon sat there totally bemused. How the hell was he to blame for those officers losing their lives? Gammon's bemusement soon turned to anger, "This is just bloody ridiculous", he thought. Gammon grabbed his coat and left for the night absolutely fuming.

His drive to Sandra's wasn't one of the most pleasant, his mind was in a whirl. Sandra came out of the house looking stunning as usual. She had on green Jodhpur type leggings with green leather ankle boots, a lemon blouse, which left nothing to the imagination, and a small cropped minx jacket. She kissed John as she got in.

"You ok John? You seem a bit down". "I will tell you about it over dinner, where do you fancy going?" "Shall we go and see Tony and Rita at the Sycamore? It's been ages since I have been there". They

# The Poet And The Calling Card

arrived at the Sycamore in Pritwich. The bar was quite busy, they had started doing Tapas on Tuesday, Wednesday and Thursday evenings, Rita informed them.

"Wish we had known Rita, we have a table booked at the Spinning Jenny". "No problem, you will have to try it another night. We have got a Spanish chef and its becoming quite popular". "I'm pleased for you both. Hi Tony". "Hey John, how are you keeping mate? I will try and have a chat with you when it calms down a bit" "No problem mate" "What can I get you two then?" "I'll have a double brandy please Rita" "For you love?" asked Rita "Best have the same please" "OK two double brandies coming straight up".

"Nice to see they have kept the interior the same, there won't be many of these pubs left soon John. Now what's a matter?" John told Sandra the full story. "How can they blame you for what happened?" "As Chief Inspector I guess I should have

## The Poet And The Calling Card

informed Kent police that this guy was a violent criminal. This will be a chance for some of my enemies to get back at me if he indeed makes an official complaint".

"John I think you are being paranoid" "I'm seriously not Sandra, I have got as far as they will allow me to go in my career and there are many in the hierarchy who would like to bring me down. Anyway let's have some more Brandy". Sandra could sense John's defence mechanism kicking in and he was on a bender, something he always did if he thought his career was coming into question. It was no good Sandra trying to stop him, it would only make it worse, at least if she took it steady she could get him home. John had four double brandies and they left for the Spinning Jenny.

"Evening Kev" "Hi John, how are you two?" "Not bad mate, yourself?". "Can't grumble, Doreen keeps me busy" "I heard that?" shouted Doreen. "Nothing said

## The Poet And The Calling Card

derogatory, my lovely" replied Kev. "I have put you on table three near the window John. You're looking very smart Sandra" "Thanks Doreen, only just got over a bout of flu" "Yeah it's going round, my niece in Micklock, was laid up for a week".

Doreen showed them to their table. "What would you like to drink?" she asked. "I'll have a white wine spritzer please" "John for you?" "I'll have a pint of Hittington and a double brandy please, Doreen". "What are we celebrating?" "Freedom Doreen, freedom!!!".

Doreen handed them the menus and went off to fetch the drinks returning a few minutes later. "Right there you go, have you decided what you want or do you need a minute" "Think we are both ready" "Ok Sandra fire away" "I'll have the Whitebait in lemon batter, followed by Steak Rossini with cottage garden vegetables, please Doreen" "I'll have King Prawns and the

# The Poet And The Calling Card

Irish stew with Stilton Cobbler, please Doreen" "Ok we will be as quick as possible" "Can I have another double brandy please?". "Bloody hell you're going for it Mr Gammon". "You ain't seen nothing yet Doreen". Doreen gave Sandra the look of "you will have some serious looking after to do tonight love".

The meals arrived and as usual were to a top standard. The problem was John was getting a lot worse for the drink and at one point he dropped the gravy boat. Doreen being the consummate professional didn't make a fuss, but Sandra had heard enough. "Come on John, I will take you home". John, by now, wasn't in a fit state so couldn't argue.

"Goodnight old lad, look after him Sandra" "We will pop in tomorrow and pay you Kev" "Not a problem, get him home safe" "Thanks Kev, I will". Luckily the pub was quiet, so at least hardly anyone had seen the state of John.

# The Poet And The Calling Card

Sandra drove down to the farm and to John's cottage. She knew the key would be under the plant pot by the front door. "Some bloody police man" she thought and smiled to herself.

Once inside she managed to get John up the stairs and onto his bed. Sandra took of his shoes and trousers and after a struggle she managed to get his shirt off and she tucked him up in bed.

The following morning Sandra was up and making toast and coffee. John came down the stairs looking dreadful. "I can't drive into work, will you take me?". "Of course how are you feeling?" "Flippin' dreadful, how did we get home? Why didn't you sleep with me?" "Well the final straw was the gravy all over Doreen's carpet in the restaurant, so I thought I'd better get you home". "Oh no, I will have to apologise". "Well you can do that tonight when you go and pay the bill" "Blimey did I walk out without paying?". "Don't worry Kev

# The Poet And The Calling Card

is cool with it, I just had to get you home John". "I'm sorry Sandra and we have a heavy day today, and now I have this disciplinary hanging over me" "Come on be positive we will get through this"

Sandra drove them both to Bixton Station. On arrival John was met by The Police Federation Officer, Jack Holmes. "Bloody hell, they weren't slow in contacting you were they Jack?" John had known Jack for many years. "Can we talk somewhere John?" "Yes go to my office at the top of the stairs and I will be with you shortly". Jack Holmes set off up the stairs while John told Sergeant Yap that Rinko Bolan and his solicitor would be here at 11.00am and to put them in interview room one and let him know. "Will do Sir".

Gammon climbed the stairs to see Jack Holmes. "Right Jack, what can I do for you?" "I am here as much as your federation officer and also as a friend John. You have made many enemies over

# The Poet And The Calling Card

the years since you have been at Bixton and the latest situation with the officers getting murdered and Chan Chi on the run again, it's just not good. I need to inform you John that a hearing is set for next Monday, it will take place here. Knowing the feeling running through the force right now, at the very least you will be demoted" "And what is the worst scenario Jack?" "You could be forced to leave the force. I told you before, way back, when that witness got murdered, a fellow officer, the retired officer and his wife. You are a maverick John and they don't like it, they really don't. I know you get the job done but it seems to always have a massive cost" "Is that it then Jack? I lay down and have my belly tickled. They are a bunch of tossers and well you know it" "John look at it sensibly, we have had witness's murdered, gangsters on the run. Your brother implicated. You and Angelina Sonjack almost murdered and that's just a few of the John Gammon

## The Poet And The Calling Card

stories. They are looking for a scape goat and that may well be you John" "Ok well thanks for nothing Jack, I will see you next Monday. Until then I have a witness to interview, so if you will excuse me". John left and Jack Holmes sat down as he brushed past him to go and interview Rinko Bolan.

"He is interview room one Sir, with Sergeant Milton and Inspector Scooper". Gammon just nodded. He entered the room and Milton announced his arrival for the tape.

"I am Chief Inspector Gammon, this is my colleague Inspector Scooper and Sergeant Milton. For the tape you are?" "I have done nothing wrong, I am not illegal immigrant" "For the tape, could you please tell me your name?" "My name is Rinko Luman from Poland". Gammon turned to the solicitor Edwin Baxter, of Baxter, Lowe and Gerrard solicitors. "Ok do you mind if I call you Rinko?" "No sir

## The Poet And The Calling Card

that is fine, I am good man" "Ok Rinko how long have you worked for the cleaning company?" "Sixteen months. I am good worker, you ask the boss man he tell you Rinko good worker" "How long have you lived in the UK Rinko?" "For almost five years" "Where did you work before?" "In Lincolnshire for Gosberton Pickers" "What was your job there?" "Mr Gammon, I am failing to see what the connection is with the girl that was attacked". Gammon ignored Baxter and carried on.

"Have you ever been in trouble in the UK? Before you answer, think carefully, Rinko because we will check?". Rinko whispered something in Baxter's ear then said "No comment" "We have checked with Polish police and you have quite a record in Poland" "No comment" "Well let me see if I can jog your memory Rinko. Our Polish colleagues tell us that you have served time for violence towards two

# The Poet And The Calling Card

women and that you served three years in prison in 2002. You were released in May 2005 and were subsequently jailed again for burglary and attempted rape, only three months after you were let out. It then appears you came to this country and the cleaning company know you as Rinko Luman. Now does that help your memory Mr Luman or is it Mr Bolan?". Baxter leaned forward and spoke quietly into his client's ear.

"My client would like to cooperate fully with you Mr Gammon" "At last we now have common sense" "My name is Rinko Bolan. When I got the chance to come to UK I was told by a friend that if I had criminal record I would not be allowed to stay and he said he knew man who could get me false papers"

"So you bought false papers to come to the UK Rinko?" "Yes that is correct Sir" "What did you pay for them?" "I pay 6,890 Zloty which is about £1,200 pounds

# The Poet And The Calling Card

Sir" "Why were you so desperate to leave Poland?" "I wanted to start new life and meet nice girl and forget past" "Have you done that?" "Yes my girlfriend Gita is having baby soon"

"Ok, so let's go back to your past" "I don't really see this is fair to my client" Baxter interrupted. "Mr Baxter, I am conducting a murder enquiry and I do feel it is relevant. You have a dislike for women, is that correct?" " No I love my Gita" "So why did you attack women in Poland and have the record you have?" "Because I was silly man, I drink a lot in those days then I take drug, just silly man Sir". At this point Rinko broke down and sobbed. "All I want is life for me, Gita and our baby, Be proper family have nice house and nice car".

Gammon was having non-of the theatre Bolan was putting on. He then produced the orange envelope. "Do you recognise this?" "No Sir, is it birthday card?" "Look

# The Poet And The Calling Card

at the writing. Is that your writing?" "No Sir" "Write the same thing on this piece of paper". It took Bolan an age to write it as if he was making sure they didn't match. "Take this to forensics Sergeant Milton, and get them to check the writing against the envelope". Milton left the room.

"Right now I am going to ask you a question and I want a straight answer, do you understand Rinko?" "Yes Sir" "Have you ever removed business cards from my office at Bixton Police Station during your time as a cleaner at this address?" "No Sir never" "Are you sure Rinko, because if you are lying this won't help your cause" "No Sir never take anything".

"Ok. Interview suspended for now. You are free to go, but I will be passing on your file to immigration and they will be in touch. Good day". And they all left the interview room. "Pass this information onto the Immigration lads Inspector" "Sir, I've just taken a call from Sir Leonard

# The Poet And The Calling Card

Marsden from the Police Federation can you call him back?" "That's all I need Gammon" thought as he climbed the stairs to his office.

Gammon phoned the number. "DCI Gammon?", said a quietly spoken voice at the other end of the phone. "Yes Sir how can I help you?" "This isn't an easy task DCI Gammon, and one I hope I don't live to regret but I have to move quickly on this" "On what Sir?" "Well you have the disciplinary meeting on Monday, in case it goes wrong, I am sending a new DCI to run the case. You will work with her until your fate is decided at your hearing. The officer who will be at Bixton tomorrow is Detective Chief Inspector Donna Fringe. She has been in charge at Cambridge for some twelve years, she apparently has parents who live in Yontgrove in a village called Conksderry".

Gammon was dumb struck "Are you judging me before my hearing Sir?" "DCI

# The Poet And The Calling Card

Gammon, your indiscretions have been laid bare by the press for many years, I have to act on that" The phone went dead. Gammon slammed the receiver down.

Gammon went downstairs and told Yap to get everybody including Forensics into the interview room now. Gammon waited for everyone to arrive. "Ok everybody some news for you all. I am no longer heading the case. That pleasure has been given to your new DCI Donna Fringe who you will meet shortly".

First to speak was Inspector Smarty. "What's this all about Sir, you aren't leaving are you?" "You may as well know the full story. You all know I have been a pain in the side of the hierarchy for some time for different issues. A few days ago the car carrying Chan Chi to Derbyshire from Kent was hijacked and both officers were murdered. I have been told I am to have a disciplinary, which speaking to the Federation Rep, doesn't look good for me.

# The Poet And The Calling Card

It will either be demotion or at worst thrown out of the force. If it's demotion then I personally have a choice on if I feel it's justified or not. In answer to your question Dave I truthfully don't know yet".

"Sir, after all you have done here at Bixton, how can they treat you like this?" "Well just a tip for you Carl, in life you make choices you can either follow the party line or you can be true to yourself. I took the latter approach and this has upset those above quite a bit over the years, but at least I can live with myself".

"Yes Wally?" "I have known you a long time John and I am sure I don't only speak for my department but for the whole station. You are and have been an exemplary officer for as long as I have known you and I find it disgraceful that they are treating you in this manner. What are the charges?" "They are basically saying I showed scant regard to the

## The Poet And The Calling Card

officers and that I didn't follow correct procedures in the line of duty" "Well I will say this and I am very sorry if I swear in front of our female officers but that is bollocks!!!"

"Look, we will close the meeting, I am expecting Donna Fringe at any time. Please give her your full support as you always have for me. She won't have asked for this position, it's been thrust upon her".

The meeting ended and Gammon went back to his office. Sandra came in and shut the door. "Are you ok John?" "Had better day's Sandra "You aren't thinking of giving up your career are you?" "Being honest, I am unsure, but it is a possibility, anyway they may make my mind up for me!!" Thank you Sandra" "I am here for you" and she smiled and left his office.

Gammon stood in deep thought when the door to his office opened and a lady

## The Poet And The Calling Card

announced she was DCI Donna Fringe. "Hi DCI John Gammon" "Yes I know who you are Mr Gammon. I am here to head up the latest case while they sort out your future".

Donna Fringe seemed a little brusque, very well dressed in a navy blue business suit with strawberry blonde hair. Gammon smiled to himself as Fringe had quite a long fringe which covered her piercing blue eyes. "Good to meet you Donna" "Good to meet you too John. Don't know much about what happened but I do know they are looking to throw the book at you. You must have truly pissed off somebody high up John?" "More than once Donna" and he smiled.

"Let's grab a coffee and I will go through the case with you" "I also need a list of officers under your command John" "Not a problem" Gammon took DCI Fringe to his office then went to fetch her coffee. As

# The Poet And The Calling Card

he stood at the coffee machine his phone rang it was Saron.

"John? Sorry to bother you. But I am going to see a medium in Micklock on Sunday night and I have a spare ticket, would you like to come?" Normally he would have said no, but he was feeling a bit beat up so he agreed. "I will pick you up at 7.00pm Sunday night, John" "Ok look forward to it Saron". Gammon took the coffee for DCI Fringe back to his office.

"Thank you John. Let me say I have heard a lot about you. Your fame spread as far as Cambridge, so I have followed your career quite closely. You have handled many highly important cases and not always through negligence things have gone wrong. I am talking about witness's being murdered or Police corruption and murders. I also have to say your affair with your Chief Constable a couple of years ago didn't help your cause". John

## The Poet And The Calling Card

was fuming inside but pleased with himself he hadn't lost it.

"If it's any consolation, as a fellow DCI, I think you are a very good copper and I know plenty at our rank who think the same, because we have all been there. You have just pissed off people right up to Home Office level. Well now you know me, do you think we can work together, now I have had my say?"

John saw his chance. "On Monday I am about to be either demoted, put on garden leave or dismissed. Now other than dismissal, the other two choices, I can decide to either go along with their decision or walk away. I am a rich man and don't do this because I need to pay the mortgage. I do it because I am a copper and a bloody good one. So in answer to your question DCI Fringe, I suggest you watch this space. Now I need to get you up to speed on all the cases and a short

## The Poet And The Calling Card

analogy of each officer currently under my command".

Donna Fringe looked shocked at Gammons answer and she sat quietly while John filled her in on the cases and staff. After Gammon had finished bringing Donna up to speed she then started to tell him her thoughts.

"Off the record John, I feel you are being treated shabbily, but sadly it is all about being politically correct these days and you have stood on a lot of toes. My hope is we work together as DCI's but if it is the case that demotion is sanctioned please don't feel that this station feels it was justified. You have many friends here and hopefully I will be counted in that circle, eventually. I am looking forward to the challenges we may face as a team".

"I appreciate your kind words Donna, but any decision I make will be for me. I know that may sound selfish but the police force

## The Poet And The Calling Card

I joined as a young man, I am not sure I like anymore, so I will be looking at my options going forward" "Well let's leave it at that for now, but promise me you will discuss things with me before making any rash decisions?" "Ok Donna and thanks for the support" "Right let's get catching criminals".

Donna left John's office and he set about his mountain of post and paperwork. Near the bottom of the pile was an orange envelope and inside was a message. "Hello Mr Gammon, I promised you a poem and a two week window to find the next victim. If you crack the poem I will tell you roughly where she is. Put a box Ad in the Micklock Globe. Just saying her name and if you are correct you will receive information where to find her. So I previously sent you a razor blade as a clue and now here is the poem".

**"Sit a while and contemplate the actions that you do.**

# The Poet And The Calling Card

Many things may alter for you and your dozy crew.

I told you I would send a clue to find this victim.

A walking trail is first to mind of that you can be sure.

My victim is young and beautiful I know this to be true.

Time is ticking now Gammon, the clock it is set, you have two weeks from this moment before she will turn blue"

The Poet

"Donna, you'd better take a look at this". DCI Fringe read the letter. "Their reference to the razor blades? I am guessing the girls name could be Steel, Wilkinson, Sharp?" "I really don't know, but Sergeant Milton is checking missing persons over the last year to see if

## The Poet And The Calling Card

anything relates to a razor blade" "Ok what about the walking trail?" "Donna the Peak District is some five hundred and fifty five miles in area and there so many walking trails" "John we have to start somewhere, let's get uniform combing the main trails round Pritwich. Which ones would you consider to be local?" "I suggest we start with the High Peak Trail at Arkwright Bobbin, follow the trail all the way to Bowlow and then back finishing in Ackbourne. That is a thirty mile trek Donna" "Ok, let's put six uniforms in a line and get them on it". "You do know its thirty miles in total?" "They can do it over two days John".

Gammon instructed Sergeant Yap to get uniform on their way to follow DCI Fringe's instructions. Donna left Gammon and he stood looking across at Losehill knowing there was a young girl out there relying on the police's ability to decipher a poem and then to find her. How sick was

## The Poet And The Calling Card

the mind of this person? While he stood looking out of his window Milton knocked on his door.

"Come in" "Sir I think I may have a lead there was one girl that was reported missing from Sheffield two months ago. Her name is Michelle Wilkinson. She is a twenty three year old graduate. She had started her career with Milicon Industries as Assistant Human Resources Officer for the company" "Do we have an address for her parents or whoever informed the police she was missing?" "Yes, it was her mother Mary Wilkinson of The Limes, Little Dropdown, Fox Houses, Sheffield". Gammon told Fringe that he was taking Milton with him to speak to the girl's parents.

On the way over Sergeant Milton tried to discuss Gammon's up and coming case.

"What do you think will happen on Monday Sir?" "Truthfully? I don't know

# The Poet And The Calling Card

Carl, and to be honest not sure whichever way it goes if my future is in policing anymore". Carl was shocked, but understood because of the injustice of it all. They arrived at Mrs Wilkinson's house. The house was quite grand, probably an eight bed-roomed house, painted white with two large stone pillars at the front door. A grey haired lady opened the door.

"Can I help you?" "Mrs Wilkinson?" "Yes", John and Carl showed their warrant cards. "May we come in?" They met a gentleman in the hallway. "Bob Wilkinson" "DCI John Gammon and Sergeant Milton, Bixton Police" "Is this about our Michelle Mr Gammon?" "Well we are unsure, I would like to take some details" "Come through". They were shown into a library.

"So Mr and Mrs Wilkinson, could you tell me the circumstances of Michelle's disappearance?" "Michelle's is our only

## The Poet And The Calling Card

child, we lost our son to meningitis thirty years ago when he was five. We never tried for any more children simply because of the pain of losing Gary. Then twenty four years ago only by chance my wife became pregnant and nine months later we had our beautiful Michelle. Michelle's built our lives back up. We could not wish to have had a kinder, more caring and honest girl Mr Gammon. It was just over two months ago. Michelle worked until seven most Fridays, she was very conscientious and driven, she was determined to be a success". "She worked in Human Resources is that correct?" "Yes she had got her Master's Degree from Durham University one of the proudest moments of our lives. She got the job with Milicon Industries almost immediately as assistant Human Resources Manager. She was so pleased Mr Gammon".

Mrs Wilkinson had not said a word the poor women seemed to be in a daze. "Did

## The Poet And The Calling Card

Michelle have a boyfriend?" "Not that we knew of, she went to Church every Sunday and would go on outings with the Church. She did have two weeks in France with a family, which was part of the church thing, but I am quite sure she didn't have a boyfriend". "By my notes you phoned South Yorkshire Police at 10.40pm on Friday September 23$^{rd}$ and Michelle had been missing for how long?" "Well she phoned home at 7.10pm that night to ask her Mum and me if we wanted a Chinese takeaway. It was a bit of a ritual some weeks Pizza some weeks Indian or Chinese takeaways, then Michelle and her Mum liked that baking program, so they would sit and watch that for two hours and I would read my classic car magazines. At first we assumed, after she had called and we decided on a Chinese take-away this week, that something else had cropped up at work. When we heard nothing, we tried to ring her, but it just went to answer phone. By 10.40pm I decided to call the

## The Poet And The Calling Card

police" "So the police were then involved" "Well sort of Mr Gammon, they basically said that she possibly had met with friends and would be home later and to call again if by tomorrow we hadn't seen her".

Gammon glanced over to Milton showing his disgust at the Wilkinson's treatment. "So have you heard from our Michelle?" "No I am sorry we are looking at all missing persons and Michelle's name came up so we are looking into this case as well".

Gammon felt sick inside thinking he may have to tell them that their daughter was a victim of the so called Poet, she clearly was their life.

"Well thank you for your time both of you and any new leads we get I will be back in touch" "Thank you Mr Gammon". Mr Wilkinson showed them out. He put his arm on Gammon. "Mr Gammon I am sorry if my wife seemed disinterested she

## The Poet And The Calling Card

is heavily sedated since the disappearance of our Michelle" "I understand Sir, I can assure you we will do our very best to find Michelle" "Thank you Mr Gammon".

Gammon and Milton drove away. "What a shitty situation Sir" "Dreadful, such a nice couple. Let's hope she has just run away and not the worst outcome that this nut case has got her somewhere. Let's go and see the Chinese Takeaway people".

As Chinese Restaurants go, the China Rose looked quite nice. Mr Wuu met Gammon and Milton. "How can I help you Sir?" "I see you have CCTV cameras". "Yes Sir". "Do you have footage for the 23$^{rd}$ September?" "Yes I have for all year" "Have South Yorkshire Police looked at the footage?" "No Sir, you first to ask". Again Gammon glanced at Milton. Mr Wuu showed them to a back room and even brought coffees for them as they set about from 7.00pm for the night of September 23$^{rd}$. They had been given a

## The Poet And The Calling Card

picture of Michelle and they started to study at 7.12pm Michelle appeared on the CCTV. Mr Wuu was also looking. "She nice lady, come at least once a month Sir". Gammon watched there was another woman waiting with a pushchair but other than that nothing. Michelle left with the Chinese at 7.24pm. The next CCTV cameras that should have picked her up didn't have any images of Michelle. I think "Michelle is our girl Carl". They thanked Mr Wuu and while Carl was driving back to Bixton. Gammon placed the advertisement in the Micklock Globe just stating Michelle Wilkinson. He then rang DCI Fringe. "Are you sure that was the right thing to do John? What if it isn't her? We will lose time" "Put this down to a John Gammon hunch Donna". Donna didn't say it but thought to herself that's why John was in front of a disciplinary because of his Maverick ways. "I will see you as soon as we get back Donna".

# The Poet And The Calling Card

It was almost 4.30pm when Gammon and Milton arrived back at the station. DCI Fringe met Gammon. "The beat lads did fifteen miles today, not found anything John, they will head back towards Ackbourne tomorrow". Suddenly John said to Milton "Come with me now". He left DCI Fringe looking bemused. "You drive Carl". "Where are we going in such a rush, Sir?" "To save a girl's life I hope". "What?" "Just drive to Slinginglow Car Park on the High Peak Trail Carl".

They arrived at the car park and Gammon jumped out of the car. By the time Milton caught up with him he was looking at a seat which had writing on it. "I knew I had seen those words before, look Carl see what it says on the seat".

**"Sit a while and contemplate the actions that you do"**

"Blimey Sir, well done" "No praise yet Carl, we haven't found her yet" "You go

## The Poet And The Calling Card

that way and I'll go this". The area was set aside for people to stop on their walk and eat their sandwiches, but this time of year it was desolate. "Sir, Sir quick". "What've you got Carl?" "This ground has been disturbed, and what is this pipe? I've got a spade in the car, Sir" "Quick as you can Carl".

They set about digging being mindful not to touch the pipe if John was correct that was Michelle's only access to air. They finally reached a wooden box, the pipe was connected to the box. John didn't know where he found the strength but he pulled the top of the box off. Inside was a girl she was quite thin and she appeared drugged, but she was alive.

"Get an ambulance now Carl and Forensics". Gammon cradled the girl in his arms until the ambulance arrived and the Paramedics got to work. "Do you need me to come with you lads?" "She is going to be fine when the drug she has taken has

## The Poet And The Calling Card

worn off and we get her on a drip". With that the ambulance sped off, it's lights flashing. Gammon went through what he and Carl had found, with John Walvin and the Forensic team.

"Carl, call Scooper, I want either her or Inspector Lee at this girls bedside until she wakes, then I want a statement". Carl did as instructed and they headed back to Bixton. Gammon phoned Fringe who had left for the evening. "Can't do you any harm John, well done. I won't see you before Monday, so good luck with the hearing". Gammon thanked her, as they arrived back at Bixton. "Well done Carl, I will see you Tuesday and we can have a de-brief. I have the disciplinary on Monday". "Good luck Sir, you should never have to be there, it's ridiculous in my mind". "Appreciate the support Carl, see you Tuesday".

John decided to have some tea at the Tow'd Man so that he could see Saron to

## The Poet And The Calling Card

arrange for Sunday's medium meeting. The ride from Bixton to the Tow'd Man was sight to behold even though it was Winter now, the Peak District held its beauty throughout the seasons. John arrived at the Tow'd Man and although Saron and Angelina had done an excellent job with the interior he felt it had lost the local feel. He thought that maybe that was progression and he was just being nostalgic.

"Hey John how are you?" "Yeah, good thanks Angelina" "Is it true they have you on a disciplinary?" "Yes, but who told you?" "Still got contact's you know. What I do know John, is that they are gunning for you". I guessed that much, Angelina". "They don't know a good copper when they see one. It's all this PC crap now, I'm glad I'm out. What you drinking?" "I'll have a pint of Blacksmith Waddle please and do you have a menu?" "There you go and there extras on the special's board".

# The Poet And The Calling Card

John flicked through the menu and decided on a dish off the special's board. "I'll try the Seared New Zealand Elk Tenderloin with Parsnip Mousselin and the winter garden vegetables please".

"Go on then ask me what it is? Everybody else has John" "Why? I know what it is Angelina" "Go on then what is it?" "It's Elk Steak with whipped parsnips" "Only you would know that smart arse" and Angelina laughed. "Is Saron working?" "Yes she is helping in the kitchen". "Just ask her to see me when she gets a minute" "Ok lover boy" and Angelina smiled.

John found himself a seat near the bay window overlooking the valley, all the lights were twinkling like carpet of stars.

Another pint later and Saron came out with his dinner. She looked beautiful even in her kitchen work clothes. John knew she would have been the one, if he had been able to commit. Saron sat with him.

# The Poet And The Calling Card

"You ok? Sorry to hear about your trouble at work" "Usual crap from above, Saron. Wow this dinner looks amazing" "Yes, there is a butcher just outside Ackbourne, who does all these exotic meats. You know, like crocodile and elk etc". "So are you doing ok with the business?" "Yeah all the guest rooms are booked almost every night with walkers. The food trade is still slow but hopefully these inventive menus will get people in. The thing is the Sloppy Quiche and the Spinning Jenny have such good reputations it is going to take time".

"Thank you for coming with me on Sunday. Do you want to drive or shall I pick you up?" "I'll drive Saron, I'm not going to be drinking much with the hearing on Monday". "Ok John, can we say 7.30pm then?". "Yes no problem" "Ok will let you get on with your dinner" and Saron got up to leave. Looking back once and smiling at John.

# The Poet And The Calling Card

'What a figure', he thought. The meal was excellent, two more pints and John headed for home but not before Angelina had spoken to him. "Who are you with now John?" "Nobody" he said. "What about Scooper?" "We go for a drink and a few nights out" "Still the same, non-committal Mr Gammon hey? Well you know where I am when you have had enough of Miss Scooper" and she smiled, flicked her hair and went off to serve a customer.

John headed home he opened his front door and on the mat was an Orange envelope. He opened it the content shocked him. "Well done John. You found Miss Wilkinson. I quite liked her, so I'm pleased you got one right. I will send you the next poem in the post, that way if our postal service is late, it gives you less time to find the victim" and it was signed off with a smiley face and the words The Poet. John left the note in the envelope on

## The Poet And The Calling Card

the kitchen table and decided he would drop it off at work Saturday morning.

How did the Poet know where he lived? This made John all the more sure that the perpetrator was local. After a good night's sleep John was up and showered and set off for Bixton. "Morning Sergeant Yap, how's things?" "The girl at the hospital still hasn't come round, so can't be a hundred percent on her identity Sir" "No problem, I have something here for John Walvin in Forensics" "Where do these nutter's come from Sir?" "Not a clue but they live amongst us that's for sure".

Gammon made his way down to the Forensic Lab, where Wally was working. As always John thought how lucky they had been finding Wally to replace Saron. "Take a look at this Wally" "Not another set of clues?" "No this time they are congratulating us on finding the girl" "What twisted people John". "Same sentiment's as Sergeant Yap mate.

# The Poet And The Calling Card

Anyway I guess there won't be any clues on it, but it's worth a look". "Good luck, for Monday, John". "Thanks Wally, I think I will need it to be honest".

John was just about to leave when he met Inspector Scooper. "Can I have a word Sir?" "Yes come to my office Sandra". They climbed the wooden stairs and went into John's office. "What's with the secrecy, Sandra?". "Not sure how to tell you this" she said. "Tell me what?" "Look, I know you have got a lot on but….." Sandra hesitated then it all came gushing out. "I'm pregnant!" "Really?" "Yes John, I am? Are you annoyed?" "Don't be daft I just don't know what to say". Sandra threw her arms round John. "Thank you for not being angry" "What do we do now Sandra?" "Well I think I am about fourteen weeks gone. I don't want to say anything yet if that's ok?" "Well yes, I guess so" "John, I won't say it's yours if you don't want me to?" "Look, let's not

## The Poet And The Calling Card

think about that at the minute" "Listen John, I have to pick Rosie up from her friend's house. Mum is taking her to Ireland on Sunday for a week. Shall we do something nice Sunday night?" "Ok call me" "Will do" Sandra pecked him on the cheek and left his office. 'Shit' he thought, 'now I have really gone and done it. Oh double crap, I'm seeing Saron tomorrow night, that will put the cat amongst the pigeons'.

John left work and decided to call and see Steve and Jo, their house was now almost done and looked like something Posh and Becks might live in. John pulled in front of the beautiful house. A large water fountain adorned the frontage of the house. As John got out of his car, Jo came running out. "John lovely to see you" and she gave him a big hug. Steve followed, "What's this? Can't afford dinner so thought you would sponge off us Porky?" and he laughed.

# The Poet And The Calling Card

"Shut up Steve. It's lovely to see you John, come on in" "Wow you two have made a fabulous job of this place". In the big hall leading to the sweeping staircase, hung a glass chandelier. "Where did you get that from?" "My sister, Tracey, you will meet her in a minute, she should be back from horse riding. She's an antique dealer John, so this chandelier came out of Lower Smeaton Hall in Gloucestershire" "That is some chandelier" "Took some bloody getting up there John, kept thinking of that script in only Fools and Horses when Rodney and Del Boy dropped one from the ceiling" "Oh yeah, that was so funny, I remember watching that episode with you in the Sycamore in Pritwich. Do you remember? We used to call Barry Grundy Granddad, because he had that big beard" "Good days hey mate". "Yeah, they were Steve". "So what you been up to? Which woman are you seeing now then mate?".

# The Poet And The Calling Card

Jo went off to make the coffee. "I'm seeing Sandra Scooper on and off. That's why I'm here to be honest, I need some advice". "What? From me? Are you having a laugh?" "Steve she is pregnant and it's mine" "Bloody hell! Now what?" said Steve. "Exactly and I am seeing Saron on Sunday night". "You are playing with fire my son". "I know that. The thing is, I was quite pleased when she told me. Do you and Jo want kids?" "Yeah we said we were going to finish the house first and then we would try. Sounds like you have beaten me to it as usual". "Listen Steve, don't say anything, not even to Jo". "My lips are sealed Daddy". "Bollocks, Steve, just because you are a Jaffa". "What's a Jaffa?" "Bloody seedless" and John laughed. John thought the world of Steve and vice versa, they had been a right pair of lads when they were teenagers. Coffee is ready boys and I have made some Bacon and Brie flatbreads so tuck in.

# The Poet And The Calling Card

John had just taken his first bit of his food so had cheese stringing from his mouth when he heard Jo's sister shout.

"Hello, where are you two?" "In the kitchen Tracey, we have somebody we want you to meet". John stood up, not realising the string of cheese was still on his chin. "Hi Tracey, I'm John Gammon". Tracey immediately started to laugh. "Do you always greet a lady with cheese hanging from your chin?" John could feel his face going red with embarrassment. He quickly wiped it off. "Sorry". "Only joking John, nice to meet you at last" and she presented her hand which John shook. Tracey had the figure of a twenty year old but he guessed she was about mid- forties.

"I'm very impressed with the chandelier Tracey". "Yeah it's a beauty isn't it?" Tracey was about five foot nine, quite striking, with blonde hair at shoulder length and big brown eyes.

# The Poet And The Calling Card

John tended to notice girls eyes first, he always thought they could tell you everything about a person. She had a blue riding jacket on with beige jodhpurs, which showed her excellent legs. "Enjoyed the ride Tracey?" "Oh yes, it was lovely. Our Jo is so lucky to live in such a lovely part of the country. So you are the famous John Gammon? and I get to meet you at last". John was already feeling uncomfortable and hadn't eaten anymore of his food in case he might get it over his chin again, and now she was calling him famous.

"Not sure about famous Tracey, maybe infamous" and he laughed. "So how long are you staying?" "Unsure at the moment John, there's a bit of a domestic with the hubby down in London. Maybe you could show me around the Peak District sometime soon?" "Yes, I would love to Tracey". Steve shot him a glance and smiled.

# The Poet And The Calling Card

"Listen you lot, I'd best make a move. Just thought I would just pop in and say hello" "Yeah more like you wanted to meet my sister in law Porky!". "Porky? Why do you call him that Steve?" asked Tracey. "And I thought I was the dumb one in this family" His flippin surname is Gammon, you know pork gammon" and he laughed. "Oh got it now. Give me call John" and Tracey handed him her business card. "Will do, speak soon" and John left.

As he drove back home John's mind wandered to the case and the thought of that poor girl's ordeal by the self-called Poet. 'How could a human being have such dreadful thoughts yet still appear to mock his actions?'.

For most of that day and night, John sat at home with a bottle of whisky and his thoughts. He was quite possibly going to be a dad; he had the disciplinary hanging over him; he no longer had any family and although a wealthy man, his only hope of

## The Poet And The Calling Card

a family was the chance to find his half-sister in France. What would she be like? He hadn't got a clue, but he was determined to find out. With the whisky now taking some effect, he decided to call a Private Detective that he knew of down in London.

"Saul Horobin, at your service" came the voice. "Saul how are you? John Gammon here" "Hey flippin heck Mr Gammon, long time no speak, I hear you work in the country now arresting sheep" and he did a loud cackly laugh. "You are correct, I do live in the Peak District, but the sheep are too intelligent to arrest Saul!!"

"So, how can I help you Mr Gammon?" "I am trying to trace somebody in France. All I have is the name of the mother" "Ok, what's her name?" "It's Maggie Else, she was quite famous in the day, but she is an older lady now, so if you find this person I want her kept out of it. The baby was born in a place called Riquier in France but was

## The Poet And The Calling Card

immediately given up for adoption" "What would her age be now John?" "I am told about thirty six or thirty seven Saul". "Do you have a name for the mother?" "I believe she passed away many years ago, so sorry no" "Ok John what are you wanting to pay? Obviously expenses and I charge £440.00 per day. So plus expenses it can rack up. How long do you want me to spend on this?" "I don't care Saul just find her please".

Saul was a little taken back usually clients would give him a time limit. "Saul, once you have found her, we will meet and I will pay you, but I want any photographs you can get to substantiate your findings. However, I do not want her contacting under any circumstances". "Understood John, you are the Piper so you call the tune".

John put the phone down wondering if he had done the right thing, what if she didn't

## The Poet And The Calling Card

want to know him? He knew deep down he had to see if he had any family left.

Feeling a little hung over on Sunday morning, from the copious amounts of whisky John had drunk, he decided to go for a walk. There had been a really heavy frost, so Hittington Dale in all its splendour, looked amazing. John walked up the first steep hill, across two fields and was just about to make his way down to Cowdale, when his phone rang, it was Donna Fringe.

"Good morning John, sorry to bother you on a Sunday, but I have just been informed from above that DI Jeanine Fairfield will be joining the team on Monday to help out. I didn't want you thinking that whatever the outcome of Monday's meeting is, that I had tried to push you out. This directive has come from above "Not a problem Donna, not sure what I am going to do, no matter the outcome" I've told you John, we need officers of your

## The Poet And The Calling Card

calibre, please speak with me before you doing anything" "Thanks for the support Donna, it's a shame our peers don't feel the same way". John cancelled the call and carried onto Cowdale.

It was almost lunchtime when he finally arrived at the Sloppy Quiche Café. "Hey John, how are you? I've not seen you for ages" "I'm good Karen, you keeping busy?" "Most nights, even now in the winter and breakfast at the weekends are unreal. We've had them queuing this morning" "How's Jimmy?" "Well that's another story, he was playing five a side last week and flippin' broke his wrist, so now we have got a young lad helping him in the kitchen" "Oh heck, I guess poor lad is in the dog house then Karen?" "He certainly is John" and she laughed. "Are you stopping for lunch or did you just pop into say hello?". "Lunch of course, can't walk passed this place without eating2 "Ok well the specials today are, Cowdale

## The Poet And The Calling Card

pie with roast potatoes, broccoli and carrots. Sweet potato quiche with a cheddar base and red onion with a garden salad or we have Sirloin steak strips in a cranberry gravy with a horseradish mash and garden peas". "I'll take the last one please Karen, and a nice strong black coffee". "Coming up Sir".

John sat by the window looking at the beautiful view all around the café. He sat contemplating, if he was to leave the force what would he do? Although he was financially secure, thanks to his Mum and Uncle Graham, he needed to be busy. He was still a young man. Karen arrived back with the biggest plateful. "Jimmy said his hand slipped with him only having one arm". "Tell him thanks Karen, that's lovely". John devoured the meal in double quick time.

"Any room for a pudding John?". "Best not Karen, I have to walk back and I am meeting Saron tonight. We are going to

## The Poet And The Calling Card

that medium thing in Micklock tonight" "Not going to ask if you two are back together again" and she laughed. "Me and Jimmy's mum are going, so I'll probably see you there".

John paid his bill, thanked Karen and left for the walk back. John arrived back at the cottage just before 5.00pm. He showered shaved and got ready to meet Saron. While he was waiting his phone rang it was Sandra. "Hey John, Mum will have Rosie if you fancy going out? I will drive because can't flippin drink now". John hesitated but knew he had to be truthful, so he told Sandra about the tickets to see the medium. "Why can't she go on her own? She is just trying to get her claws into you John" "It's not like that, she thinks Annie Tanney might get in touch, all nuts I know, but I do owe her that". "Ok, whatever, I will speak to you tomorrow after your case. Good luck" and she cancelled the call. Saron was pipping

## The Poet And The Calling Card

outside so John locked the kitchen door and went to the car. Saron had made a real effort, she had on cream coloured, tight trousers with brown high heels and a bottle green silk blouse, she looked a million dollars.

"Evening Mr Gammon, this brings back memories". John laughed unsure of what the reply should be. "What are you hoping for tonight Saron?" "Well it would be nice if dad came through. What about you?" "Not sure what to expect to be honest".

They arrived at Micklock Reading Rooms, there were about three hundred people packed into room five. After a short talk by the host she introduced Lillian Campbell, a lady in her late seventies John thought. Lillian had a scouse accent which was very pronounced. She spoke quite quietly.

"I realise tonight some of you have been to my experiences before and some of you I

## The Poet And The Calling Card

have no doubt are first time people and maybe are sceptical. Before I try and contact anybody, let me tell you all monies taken for the sale of the tickets are given to a children's charity. The only money not given to the charity, is for the hire of the room and the facilities. I personally take no money from my experiences thank you".

Lillian sat for a good five minutes, the room was in silence other than the odd rustling, as the silence became eerie. Suddenly Lillian spoke. "Is there a Gary in the room?" Nobody answered. "Sorry this lady is saying Gareth, she is telling me off for saying Gary". One man put his hand up. "You are Gareth?" "Yes" he replied. "Well I have a lady here and she says it's time you visited Arthur, just a minute, yes Arthur. Do you know an Arthur?" "Yes, he is my father" "Why is this lady telling you to see Arthur?" "I think the lady in question is my mum, Dina Chutch". "She

## The Poet And The Calling Card

is telling me you are correct. Why would she want to you to go and see your father?" "My father left us when I was seven. My mum always loved him. I have never been to see him, but my uncle said he is in a home and that he is asking after me". "Ok Gareth, we won't ask you why he left but I am assuming you have been hurt, your Mum is saying to me that you need to forgive him before it's too late. Will you go and see your father?" "If Mum wants it, then yes, I will" "She said thank you Gareth. I'm afraid she has gone now Gareth". Gareth sat down and the room fell into silence again.

"I have a lady with an Irish accent, she says Saron still loves you John". Saron looked at John. John didn't know what to say. "Does that mean anything to anyone? Do we have a John in the room?". Saron poked John but he was reluctant to stand up. "I am getting her name, I think she is saying Annie. Yes Annie. She said you are

## The Poet And The Calling Card

a good man, but sometime soon where you lay your hat must be your home John". Lillian spoke, "John I have a strong feeling who Annie is talking about is in this room, but I understand if you wish not to get up in front of everyone. She is speaking again. She is telling me that you saw heaven when she was holding your hand in the hospital and she said the world is a better place with you in it and you must not stop doing what you do. Annie is a very strong lady and she says she will guide you John, but you must listen to what she is telling you. There are jealous people trying to ruin your life, you must be strong and stand up to them and she will help you John. Sorry John Annie is fading. If whoever that message was for please listen to what Annie has said" "Ok we are going to take a break for ten minutes"

"Come on Saron I want to go?". "Why John?". "I will tell you, let's go to the

# The Poet And The Calling Card

Spinning Jenny" "Ok Mr Gammon your call but I am driving".

Once in the Spinning Jenny they found a quiet corner. "John I have loved being with you tonight, why did we split?" "Look Saron, that shook me up a bit tonight. If that was indeed Annie Tanney and I have no reason to believe differently, then it changes what I was thinking about the disciplinary on Monday" "What do you mean?" "Well I think she was telling me there are greater forces trying to bring me down? I was seriously considering leaving the force, no matter what the outcome of the meeting" "Really? I am surprised it's your life John" "I know but I am worn down by the red tape. I didn't join the police force for all this PC crap Saron".

"She said you saw heaven, did you?" "I never told anyone, not even Annie, for fear of ridicule but yes I think I did". "Explain John" "I remember a really

## The Poet And The Calling Card

bright light and I was like walking through what can only be described as a cloud tunnel, in the distance I could see Angels and they were pointing I looked round and I could see like a black ghost behind me. They looked like the cartoon 'Casper the friendly ghost', only all black. I started to run towards the three Angels, I kept looking behind me but they never seemed to follow me. Once I arrived at the Angels they disappeared and I was in a garden. My brother Adam was stood with Ellie and it looked like they were getting married. I tried to speak to them. Adam turned and looked at me and said, "Go home John, it's not your time, don't be afraid you are strong and people need you". I knew I had to turn back and face the demons that had been behind me. As I walked towards them, they surrounded me. I could hear them saying "Take. Take". I stood up to them and said I am going home and they like melted away. The next thing I knew was I was coming

## The Poet And The Calling Card

round, the pain had gone and Annie was holding my hand. Lillian tonight wasn't a fake, she was for real, because nobody knew what I told you not even Annie".

"John that is amazing. Now what?" "I am going to take whatever they throw at me, stay put and prove them all wrong Saron" "That's more like the John I love and respect. Whoops, I said that word again, the one that frightens you" "What's that?" "Love. You know commitment word" "Want another drink Saron?" She smiled at John, her beautiful teeth lighting up her face.

John made his way to the bar. Kev was beaming. "Ok what is making your day Kev?" "Just smiling to myself, if ever a guy should have been James Bond, it's you. They bloody fall at your feet" said Kev. "Give up with all that crap", replied John. "I'm telling you! Last night I overheard Jo's sister-in-law telling Jo how she fancied the pants off you" "Now I

## The Poet And The Calling Card

know you are telling porkies, I only met her Saturday morning" "Yes I know, she said. They were in Saturday night that's when I overheard the conversation". "You do talk some crap Kev, it's that bloody dickie bow, it strangles the oxygen to your brain". "We'll see, but bet I am proved right". "Tell me something, since you split with Saron, have you heard if she has been out with anyone else?" "No but she has been busy with the pub. My Doreen said when you split, that Saron would not let you go. Hey Doreen come here, what did you tell me" "You owe me a day off?" she replied. "No about Saron and John?" "Well I was right, they would be back together". "Well you are both wrong. This was a one off, now give me my drinks" and he laughed. "We will see my lovely" "Thanks Doreen" and John returned to Saron.

"You took your time". "Just Kev giving me stick about being out with you, he

## The Poet And The Calling Card

reckons we will be back together" "Well I wouldn't say no to that John". John just smiled and stayed non-committal knowing the situation with Sandra.

"Are you coming back to the Tow'd Man for a nightcap John?" "Be rude not to I guess". They finished their drinks said goodnight to Kev and Doreen. Kev gave John a cheeky wink as they headed out for the Tow'd Man.

"Angelina is leaving at 11.00pm, she is taking Monday and Tuesday off. She's going to see Cats in London, with a friend from when she worked down there, so we have the pub to ourselves once she leaves".

"Hi Angelina have we been busy?" "No, it's been dead tonight, last customer left about ten minutes ago, so I would lock up if I were you. I'm going to get off" "Nice to see you John" and she smiled and tweaked John's buttock as she left.

# The Poet And The Calling Card

Another couple of Brandies and John was now in single happy mode with the beautiful Saron in full tease mode. "Shall we go upstairs John?" This was an offer John could not resist, as he followed Saron's stunning figure up the stairs. Once in the bedroom, it was like they had never been apart, their love making was on a different level from anytime previous. Once their lust was satisfied, they lay in each other's arms.

"I want us to be together again John, I think about you every waking hour" "Saron it's complicated" he said. "Sandra isn't for you John, it's just lust, it's time to admit to yourself". How could John even begin to tell her that Sandra was carrying his baby? The conversation about their relationship carried on during the night before they both eventually fell asleep.

John's hearing was at 11.00am. John woke at 8.30am along with a bit of a headache. Saron was up and cooking breakfast, so he

## The Poet And The Calling Card

quickly showered then went downstairs. "Get this inside you John, you have a long day ahead of you. Just promise me you won't do anything silly" "I probably would have but it looks like Annie Tanney saved the day for me again".

John Gammon arrived at Flagg Hal,l a Tudor mansion house used for corporate events. John's rep met him in the hallway. "John they are going to throw the book at you and to be honest a lot of it is not defendable on your part" "Look I get results" said John, "But you don't do it by the book John" "DCI Gammon" a voice said. "Yes, that's me." "Follow me Sir". The tall burly man led John and the Police rep to a large room. John was unsure what to expect, there were two chairs one for him and one for the rep. Opposite the long oak table there were six people, two women and four men.

"Ok DCI Gammon, I will outline the charges against you and you will be asked

## The Poet And The Calling Card

questions by the panel with regard to your conduct".

"The charges are as follows.

1) You have a maverick approach to policing which over the last few years has led to officers losing their lives.
2) You have scant regard for authority and the need for disciplined policing.
3) You have had indiscretions with fellow officers some who hold a higher ranking than yourself."

"Point one. Mr Gretton will outline the charge then you will be able to answer" "Mr Gretton" "DCI Gammon, a suspect in a murder case in the Peak District was arrested attempting to leave the country at Dover. You were informed that two uniformed police officers were escorting said suspect. You failed to inform Kent police of the serious nature of the crimes

# The Poet And The Calling Card

this man was allegedly involved in. Because of your action's two police officers were killed that afternoon and the suspect escaped is that correct?"

"Your comments are correct and in hindsight I should have contacted Kent police and informed them that Chan Chi was a dangerous man. I am not wishing to apportion blame and as commanding officer at Bixton I should have and I apologise unreservedly to the Kent Police Force and to the families of the two officers". All the time he was saying this he knew that Sergeant Carl Milton had been at fault by not informing him of how Chi was being transported but he could not say anything.

"With regard to point two. Sarah Barkham, from Nottinghamshire Police, Sarah".

"DCI Gammon, all serving officers and certainly those with authority over lower

## The Poet And The Calling Card

ranking officers, have a duty of care. You have blindly had total disregard for this and at times have been such a maverick. I believe, looking at previous case notes you have actually endangered police officers lives and this is not acceptable at any level. What would you like to say Mr Gammon?".

"I refute that allegation. I have always taken my responsibilities and duty of care to all my fellow officers very seriously. Sometimes you have to make snap decisions in the field and sometimes the risks are greater than the rewards but I would never, knowingly, put any of my officers or the public in danger". "Thank you DCI Gammon". John could sense Barkham was out for blood so this wasn't going to end well.

"With regard to point three on the agenda, Beryl Butterley from Newcastle Police, will give her opinion". Gammon knew of Butterley, she was a rising star in the

## The Poet And The Calling Card

North and was basically a man hater so this was going to get nasty.

"DCI Gammon, with regard to point three your indiscretions with fellow officers are known. I believe you were passed over for promotion on more than one occasion. Newspapers made you somewhat of a star on some case but with the glory there is also a downside. Once on your pedestal they started to chip away at you culminating in various stories and pictures of your love life being splashed all over the media, thus discrediting Derbyshire Police, which is plainly and morally incorrect for a serving officer of her majesty's police to be involved in".

"Thank you, Beryl. You may speak now Mr Gammon".

"First of all can I say in my defence, none of us choose to fall in love, it happens. How it was all reported was grossly incorrect some of the pictures that showed

## The Poet And The Calling Card

me partying into the early hours, while girls were being murdered, were totally untrue. Those pictures were taken at a family wedding some three years earlier. All the cases I have been involved in, both I, and my team, have worked tirelessly for many hours to get convictions. My private life should be just that. So I know you will make your own decision on my career but know this. I love my job and I also think I am damned good at it". The rep said nothing, much to John's annoyance.

"Mr Gammon we will take a break if you wish to get some lunch and we will reconvene at 2.00pm, thank you".

They got up and left the room, the rep turned to John. "Do you fancy an Italian? I know a cracking place round the corner". "Let me tell you what I want, I don't want or need you sat next to me at 2.00pm this afternoon for the verdict. You have not helped in anyway in my defence, so the best thing you can do is go away and

## The Poet And The Calling Card

crawl back under whatever stone you came from" and Gammon got up and walked out of the room leaving the rep open mouthed.

John grabbed a coffee and sat in the Victorian park watching the ducks slipping and sliding on the iced up pond. He knew this was going to be bad and he feared the worst.

2.00pm came and it was time for the decision. Gammon was told to stand. Nobody commented on the absence of the federation rep, think they all thought he was useless.

"Detective Chief Inspector John Gammon, it is my duty as chair of this committee to tell you of the decision of the panel. We have listened with interest at your defence and we have no doubt you are a loyal police officer and some of this panel do realise the pressures of the job can sometimes create bad decision making.

# The Poet And The Calling Card

We are also aware that you have run Bixton Police Station without a Chief Constable present and for that reason, although I have to say it was a close call, you will not be asked to leave the force. You will, however, be demoted to a Detective Inspector as from today".

John felt relief, but also anger, but he kept his counsel.

"Your future conduct will be monitored for the next twelve months and should any of today's findings be revisited, serious consequences will be put in place. Thank you DI Gammon".

Gammon stared at Sarah Barkham he knew she had put the boot in. she in turn smirked at John as she went past.

There was only one place John Gammon knew at a time like this and that was the Spinning Jenny and his mate Kev. On the way his mobile rang it was Donna Fringe.

# The Poet And The Calling Card

"Very sorry to hear the result John, but better than expected from the bits I heard on the grapevine. You are staying on aren't you?" "Yes I am Donna, and thanks for the call" "Well my call has two reasons, one to hopefully hear you say you are staying with the team and the second one to say Michelle Wilkinson has just come round and she is ok. No long term damage other than the trauma of course. I wondered if you would like to inform her parents that their daughter is safe and well and can be visited at Bixton hospital". "Ok Donna, I will go now and thanks for the support". Gammon knew Donna had asked him to do this to get him back into policing and not being down and thinking about things.

On the drive to Sheffield John felt good. Generally it would be to tell some poor family that there son or daughter had been found dead and all the heartache that would bring. He pulled up at the

# The Poet And The Calling Card

Wilkinson home and was met by Mr Wilkinson John could tell by the look on his face that he wasn't expecting good news. "DI Gammon, may I come in Sir" "Sorry if the house is a little untidy Mr Gammon" and he broke down. "Hey Mr Wilkinson, it isn't bad news we have found your daughter". Gammon put his arm on Bob Wilkinson's shoulder. The poor man's face was ashen. "Are you ok?" "Yesterday I took a call from Julie, Mary's sister. I had sent her down to Dorset for a few weeks. Mary had apparently wandered off on the pretence of going for a walk. My sister-in-law got worried after five hours when she hadn't returned. The police were called and she was found dead on some railway lines she had committed suicide Mr Gammon"

"Bob I am so sorry. We have found Michelle she is in hospital in Derbyshire. She is a little fragile but other than what her abductor put her through, she is ok. Do

## The Poet And The Calling Card

you drive Bob?" "Yes I do Mr Gammon". "Well look, this is the address of the hospital and the ward Michelle is on. Would you like a liaison officer to come over and talk with you?" "No, I will be ok I have two sisters close by who are on their way. Mary was so drugged up on medication, she didn't know what she was doing" "I am so sorry Bob I really am. I know this is no consolation, but I will get this evil man that has put your family through so much. I promise you".

Just then Bob's two sisters's arrived. "Here is my card if you need anything". John realised his card said DCI and not DI, as he was now, but he was sure that would not matter to poor Bob. The drive back to the Peak district was so much worse than how he felt going over. He kept thinking maybe the tribunal were right, what if he hadn't have waited for Michelle to come round, maybe Mary Wilkinson would not have done what she

## The Poet And The Calling Card

did. John phoned Donna. "Just to keep you in the loop Donna" and he proceeded to tell her the tragic news about Michelle's mother. "Oh how sad John, that poor man gets his daughter back then loses his wife, all because of some evil person. I will see you tomorrow John, we need to interview Michelle" "Nothing came back on the latest envelope, I have just spoken with John Walvin in Forensics. I am of the opinion this man or woman has planned this for a long time. I don't think they have just bought these envelopes" "Why wouldn't they use a common white envelope?" "They would be almost impossible to trace". "I think you're right Donna" "Ok, have a nice evening, John and we will talk in the morning".

With it being almost 5.00pm and John not really wanting to bump into Sandra after the day he had had, he decided to head for the Spinning Jenny and a pint with Kev.

# The Poet And The Calling Card

The drive from Bixton was a bit treacherous the roads were like glass. With all the cut backs the Council hadn't been doing as much gritting as previous years. He drove down the valley from Bixton, perhaps being a little Maverick as those idiots at the disciplinary would say, using the back roads but hey, that was John Gammon he thought. In his mind he was remembering Christmas last year and how much he thought of Saron. He never thought there was a glimmer of hope that they would get back together, then Sandra tells him she is pregnant and Saron rings him out of the blue and he spends the night with her.

'My life really is a rollercoaster' he thought. He pulled into the car park at the Spinning Jenny. It was in darkness, other than a few candles flickering in the windows. John walked into the bar area. The pub was quite busy, a few lads were playing darts. Apparently they call in after

## The Poet And The Calling Card

work from Hittington Quarry and Spencer Fabrication at Lingcliffe.

Kev was beaming. "How are you tonight young John?" "Had better days mate, but you look like life is treating you well" "Well the pub is busy, those lads will have a gallon each most nights it's become a bit of ritual, this darts competition. We have got fifty five booked in the restaurant for eight o clock, Bixton Rotary Club Christmas dinner" "Bit early for that mate?" "It's what they do John now, most companies have it either early December or late January. It's better for us because it staggers it over the Christmas period. Also I'm pleased you came in" "Why's that?" "We are organising a mini break, only three days, are you going to put your name down and whichever piece of arm candy you would like to bring?" "Not sure Kev, I've a lot on at work and my love life is a bit complicated" "Bloody hell John, when isn't it?" and Kev laughed making his red

## The Poet And The Calling Card

dickie bow jump up and down on his Adam's apple.

"Let me get you a beer then we can talk" "Ok mate a Pedigree please". Kev pulled the pint. Joni appeared. "Here's my little saviour" "Thanks Kev, that was a nice compliment" "We are going to be really busy tonight Joni". "I would sooner have it that way. Hi John how are you?" "Good thanks, Joni. Kev is trying to talk me into going on that break to Barcelona" "Why not? I'm going" she said. "What, you and Carl?" "No me and Carl are on a break" "Oh sorry to hear that" "Think we have too much grief binding us John". "Who else is going on this trip Kev?" "Jo and Steve, Jack and Shelley, Bob and Cheryl, Me and Doreen, Joni. Not sure if Sheba Filey and her new bloke are coming, she is letting me know tonight" said Kev. "When is it?" asked Joihn. "This weekend" "Oh what the hell, put me down for a place." "Just you John?" "Yes" "Thought you

## The Poet And The Calling Card

would be taking Sandra or even Saron John?" John smiled at Joni they both knew what the smile meant.

"Hey Porky" a bellowing voice came from round the stone pillar. "Hey up Stevie boy". "Come and join us, I have my lovely sister in law with me and Jo". John paid Kev for the trip then went round the corner to sit with Steve, Jo, and Tracey Rodgers.

"So they are leaving you back here while they go off to Barcelona then Tracey?" "Well they were" she said, and Tracey got up and asked Kev to book her on. "Looks like the Gammon magic is working on your sister Jo". "Give over Steve, you are always embarrassing John." "I'm used to it Jo but thanks for the concern."

Tracey came back and she had bought another round of drinks with her. They could hear a commotion in the bar. "What's all that noise?" "Some women dressed in a frog suit collecting for

# The Poet And The Calling Card

Swinster Pensioners Christmas Dinner". "I know who that is Steve." "Bet I can guess before you!" and they all blurted out "Carol Lestar" On hearing that, the frog appeared with the charity bucket. "Come on you tight gits, it's for a good cause." They all put a tenner in but Carol would not give up on John. "Make it a twenty pound note or I am staying here with you all night and it will cost you more in drinks my lovely copper".

John added a twenty pound note to the tenner he had already put in the bucket and Carol thanked him and carried on round the pub. "Say what you like about Carol but she has a heart of gold and she enjoys life." "Yep agree Steve she is a lovely lady always has been. She used to babysit me and Adam when we were little. I remember I stayed one night and we set the duvet alight, do you remember?. "Oh yeah we found that box of matches and we decided to toast some marshmallows so

## The Poet And The Calling Card

you sneaked down and got a frying pan and we made a fire in the frying pan. All was going well until the pan got too hot, the duvet was dangling off the bed and it set alight." "Yeah Carol was brilliant that night she put the fire out changed the duvet and told mum I had been sick on it and insisted that she washed it with her being in charge. She even bought a new one from Bixton exactly the same, what a star".

Jo and Tracey were falling about laughing "You were a right bloody pair when you were young." "I can vouch for that" Kev shouted from behind the bar.

Tracey and John were flirting all night and at the end of the night he pecked her on the cheek and said he would see them all at the weekend. As he was leaving Joni shouted him over. "Shall I do a flask and some sandwiches for Friday?" "If you want to." "I know you don't like salad cream" and she laughed. "Good memory

## The Poet And The Calling Card

there mate." Joni blushed as John walked away.

The following day John arrived at Bixton and was introduced to DI Jeanine Fairfield by Donna Fringe. "John I am going to have a meeting in the incident room, I need everyone to know your situation and how I want the investigation to be carried out, moving forward are you ok with that?" "Not a problem Donna, I would imagine the rumours are rife anyway." "Oh by the way I am taking Friday off, if that's ok?" "Don't see why not John. Meeting at 9.30am then in the incident room" Jeanine smiled at John and he carried on up to his office. It was a good job the sign on the door had never been altered to Chief Inspector Gammon perhaps it was always meant to be this way.

The second envelope down sent shivers down Gammons spine. He carefully opened it.

# The Poet And The Calling Card

*Dear John,*

*Well done on finding Michelle, I hope she is fine, clearly she was meant to be saved. Now it's time for number three so I hope you have your clever head on because the clock ticks from now.*

*"Under the spreading Chestnut Tree our third victim she stood. Now she fights for breath and no longer is she stood. That metal wire that holds her tight and slowly cuts her neck will not allow movement. Now this envelope was sent.*

*Finally my friend the clue to this pretty girl's name you find the A in apple and the N in No but all the other letter's I hope you will never know.*

*Good luck Mr Gammon the clock is ticking"*

# The Poet And The Calling Card

## *The Poet*

The writing was identical to the others, very scrawled writing, did this mean the Poet was ill - educated?

Gammon took the envelope and letter to the meeting. DCI Fringe was stood at the front. "Ok we are all here, first of all you are probably aware I have been installed at Bixton to head up the investigation into the murders that are been carried out by the self-called Poet."

"It doesn't really matter what we as a team think about Di John Gammon and how he has been treated by our peers. Our job is to focus on serving the public to the best of our abilities. From today the decision has been taken that former DCI John Gammon will be a Detective Inspector." There were quite a few mumblings coming from the mouths of DI Lee and DI Smarty. "I know how you all feel but I have a job to do and anybody that feels they can't accept the

## The Poet And The Calling Card

decision or feels they can't work with me, I suggest you speak up now". John gestured to speak. "Yes John?" "Can I just say I very much appreciate your support and I love my job, I will be giving DCI Fringe every bit of support I can and I want to work alongside you all. We have a great team, let's get this freak that is causing so much harm in our communities".

"This morning, in my post, was another Orange envelope" and John read out the contents to everyone.

Donna started marking up clues on the wipe board. Chestnut Tree; wire; then A and N. "Right what do we all think, Scooper?" "I don't think the Peak District has many chestnut trees in woodlands, they are found in parks etc." "Why is that Scooper?" "They were brought over here from Turkey in the sixteenth century, so are not an indigenous tree in Britain." "Interesting, so where do we look?" "I

## The Poet And The Calling Card

would say parks, maybe churches Ma'am, I know there is one in Pritwich Church because we used to get conkers from it when we were kids."

"Ok let's take a look at that, seeing that the first victim was found at the side of the church. Let's see if we have any connections between the girls. John, I would like you to interview Michelle Wilkinson" "Will do" "Milton you work with DI Gammon on this. Scooper and Smarty, let's find every Chestnut Tree in the Peak District, catalogue them, then with uniform I want each one visiting, look for disturbed ground."

"Finally, I would like you all to meet our new colleague DI Jeanine Fairfield. She has been decorated twice for bravery, I am sure doesn't want me to go on about it but she is a very capable officer. Di Fairfield, shadow Di Gammon, you will learn a lot from him. Ok thank you everybody, let's get going we have two weeks to find this

## The Poet And The Calling Card

poor girl. I will give this to Forensics, but we have found nothing on the others however, you never know we might get lucky."

They all left, John, Jeanine and Carl went to Bixton Hospital to interview Michelle Wilkinson. "How do you know Donna Fringe Jeanine?" "I was a sergeant under her in Liverpool about seven years ago. She is a good copper, expects high standards but I've always found her fair and supportive. Sorry about your situation and have to say a bit surprised everyone has heard of John Gammon!!" "Maybe that's the problem Jeanine." They arrived at Bixton Hospital, Michelle was sat up in bed, her father by her bedside. John introduced himself, DI Fairfield and Sergeant Milton. Michelle thanked John for saving her life. He in return said his condolences on the loss of her mother.

"Do you feel up to talking about your ordeal Michelle?" "Yes, I want this person

## The Poet And The Calling Card

caught Mr Gammon." "Ok well Sergeant Milton will be taking notes. Can you run through the night you were abducted?". "I called Mum as I left work to get Mum and Dad's Chinese order." "Was there anybody else in the shop?" "I can't recall. I waited for my Chinese then thanked Mr Wuu and left the shop. I remember walking down Fitzwilliam Street, it is well lit there. Dad said I always have to walk down there, even if it takes a bit longer." "Yeah we have microwaves now I tell her." "Thank you Mr Wilkinson." "I know Dad won't be pleased but instead of going across to Hunger Street. I tend to take the short cut across some waste land,where the old Woolworths used to be because my car is parked at the other side. All I can remember after that was everything going black. When I came round I was in what seemed like a cellar, it smelt damp. I could not see anything because I was not allowed to take the thing off that was over my head. My hands were tied behind my

## The Poet And The Calling Card

back and my feet were tied to the chair at least think it was a chair. The person that kept me prisoner only came once a day, to feed me and they spoon fed me. But they never lifted the thing over my eyes. When the person walked, I think they had a limp. You know how people with limps tend to drag their feet Mr Gammon. Every day after I was fed, the person would go somewhere in the room and I could just hear them mumbling. It sounded like the Lord's Prayer but I can't be certain. When I was put in the ground, I knew nothing. He put something in my arm and I remember being sleepy and lifeless. After that, I don't know how long later, I remember feeling that it was hard to breath and it was dark everywhere. I could just see a small shaft of light. My mouth was taped up so I was trying to breathe through my nose." At this point Michelle broke down her father comforted her, "You are safe now Michelle."

# The Poet And The Calling Card

Gammon could feel the anger running through his body this twisted person had caused such grief to this family.

"Michelle I am sorry to ask you this, have you got a boyfriend?" "No Mr Gammon." "You are a pretty girl, so why is that?" "To be honest with you I spend so much time on church and charity work, it's never bothered me." "Has anybody asked you out from work?" "A guy in the quality lab asked me out last Christmas." "Can we have his name?" "He is a nice man Mr Gammon, I don't want to cause him any trouble." "I need to eliminate him from our enquiries." "His name is Jamie Dale, he is a quality engineer at work. His wife ran off with a car salesman three years ago and he has had a really hard time." "Ok Michelle, other than Jamie, was there anyone else? Anyone from Church, perhaps?" Michelle answered very quickly, "No Mr Gammon". Gammon thought this a little odd, was she hiding

## The Poet And The Calling Card

something? Or perhaps she was embarrassed in front of her Dad.

"Ok Michelle, here is my card if you remember anything else, anything at all, no matter how small call me please, it may be important." "Ok Mr Gammon." "Thank you for saving my daughter Mr Gammon, I will be for ever in your debt." DI Fairfield looked across at Milton in admiration at how well thought of Gammon was.

They arrived back at Bixton and Gammon updated DCI Fringe on Michelle's statement. "Do you think she was seeing somebody from the Church?" "Not sure Donna, but she was very quick to deny anything." "Maybe we should get a list of the Churches she has visited and the charity days, or visit's she has had and with who." "Fully agree Donna, but I would just give the kid a week, she has had a harrowing ordeal and maybe Inspector Scooper could go and see her in

## The Poet And The Calling Card

a week's time." "Yes, I think you are right, I will fill Scooper in and she can go in a week's time."

"I will take DI Fairfield with me to speak with Jamie Dale at Milicon Industries, they are in Beaumont, just inside Derbyshire, so no need to bother Yorkshire police it's our patch."

Gammon and Fairfield arrived at Milicon at 4.00pm, they entered the reception and after showing their badges they were asked to take a seat whilst Lori Hover, head of Human Resource, could see them.

A woman in her late fifties, with long grey hair, the sort that annoys you, when you see women that look like ex hippies that have let their hair go all straggly. "How can I help you detectives?" "Do you have a private room?" "Yes, come to my office." They followed the lady down a

## The Poet And The Calling Card

rabbit warren of corridors until finally arriving at her office.

"Is this about poor Michelle? We have just had a collection for her, poor girl, and then her father said he had lost his wife also. They are such a lovely Christian family." "Well we are following up our inquiries we would like to speak with a Mr Jamie Dale." "You don't think Jamie is involved in this, surely not?" "We are just following a line of inquiry. We will need you to leave the office once you have fetched him" "Not a problem Mr Gammon, I can wait outside until you are finished."

Jamie Dale entered the office. "Mr Dale?" "Yes" "DI Gammon and DI Fairfield." "What's this about? I never threatened Christine or her boyfriend, I just want to see my kids." "This isn't about you and your wife, but I will just say, do not go around threatening anyone. Now I believe you know Michelle Wilkinson?" "Yes that's correct." "We are also led to believe

## The Poet And The Calling Card

you may have asked her out." "Yes I did, but only for a drink and a bite to eat. That's not a crime is it? I'm single now and so is she." "I am not implying it is a crime Mr Dale. As you are aware Michelle was brutally attacked and she only just survived her ordeal. Can you tell me your movements over a week last Friday?" "I finished work at 6.00pm, I called in town for a quick drink then went home." "Did you speak with anyone in the bar?" asked Gammon, "Only the girl behind the bar, when I ordered my drink." "What time did you leave the pub? Which pub was it, incidentally?" "The Sir William, Sir" "Where is that?" "It's on Fitzwilliam Street".

The DCI glanced at Gammon. "What time did you leave the pub?" "About 7.30pm. They had the telly on and Coronation Street came on, my missus used to watch it all the time so I knew it was 7.30pm." "So you left the pub, then what?" "I went

## The Poet And The Calling Card

home." "What, you drove home?" "It's ok, I only had one and a half pints." "Ok, so the barmaid at the pub, do you know her?" "No." "What did she look like?" She had long dark hair and heavy makeup, bit like a Goth, I think that's the correct term." "Ok Mr Dale, we may need to question you further, so don't leave the country." "All this, because I asked a girl out for a beer? Bloody incredible!" and he got up and left. Lori Hover came back in. "He looked annoyed as he left Mr Gammon?" "Yes it appears to me that he has a bit of a temper. Thank you that will be all." "Let me show you out."

They got back in the car. Jeanine put Fitzwilliam Street into the Sat Nav, "Let's go and talk to the Goth barmaid." The pub was two point seven miles away. It stood in a typical urban decayed area, possibly a nice pub in its day, but very shabby now. They walked in and the place was full the beer was £2.50 a pint so all the local soaks

## The Poet And The Calling Card

were in there. Luckily the girl behind the bar was the Goth. Gammon ordered two drinks then asked the girl if she remembered a guy with blonde curly hair coming in and drinking one and a half pints then leaving last Friday. "He would have been about twenty eight?" "Bloody hell, I serve hundreds of people here, on a Friday." She said. Gammon had noticed that she had tattoos and he remembered that Jamie Dale had a skull and cross bone tattoo between his thumb and finger.

"This guy had a tattoo a skull and cross bone." "Oh you mean Pirate!. We call him Pirate, he has been coming in here for about three months and he is always trying to chat up the girls behind the bar. He's bloody odd him. Why what has he done?" "Nothing, that I am aware of. He said he left at 7.30pm." "Not sure about that, I know Corrie was on because my Nan comes in for half a Guinness and she sits and watches Corrie. I went back to clear

## The Poet And The Calling Card

the bar and he had gone, so yeah about 7.30pm I guess." "Ok thanks, sorry what was your name?" "Michaela Burton." "I will leave you my card. If you think you may have missed anything, give me a call." "I will handsome" she said. "Bloody hell John, she had the hot's for you." "Don't think I am her type Jeanine." "Could have fooled me" and she laughed.

"Let's get back to the station and see how everyone else is getting on." It was a typical Bixton winter's day, very cold with snow forecast for the afternoon. "Where are you living Jeanine?" "At the moment I am staying at the Spinning Jenny in Swinster, but I am going to look at a place in Ardwalk. Somebody the landlord recommended, they have a barn conversion on a long lease if I like it." "Will that be Jack and Shelley Etchings by any chance?" "Yes that's correct, do you know them John?" "Yes, Jeanine they're good friends of mine." "I haven't been to

## The Poet And The Calling Card

Ardwalk yet, is there a pub and shops?" John laughed. "Nearest you will get to a pub is Jack's home brew and as for shops you might be able to get a dozen eggs from one of the farms. It's not classed as a village more, it's a hamlet Jeanine. I am sure you will like it though all nice people that live up there and it's a proper community."

Gammon reported back to Donna and she called a meeting to discuss any developments.

"Ok everybody, it appears that our Mr Jamie Dale has a concrete alibi, a pub full of people and he was in the pub at 7.30pm on the night of the abduction. Yes DI Scooper?" "How were they so sure he was there at 7.30pm? In a busy pub Ma'am?" "Apparently Coronation Street starts at 7.30pm and the barmaid said he didn't leave until just after then. Yes, DI Smarty?" "Ma'am, Coronation Street was on at 7.00pm on that Friday, something to

## The Poet And The Calling Card

do with an Engineers strike. ITV was off from 7.30pm, so they moved Corrie forward, with that being the most popular." "Really DI Smarty, can we check that out? and if that's the case I want this guy bringing back in with his solicitor and I want a search warrant while we have him in custody.

DCI Fringe was very concise on what she wanted, John could see she was a good Detective Chief Constable. "Ok, now what about the third potential victim and the poem, any ideas? Yes Scooper?" "Myself and DI Smarty have located one hundred and sixty seven places where Chestnut trees are situated in the Peak District. From those, twenty three are in two woodland areas, both in the High Peak. Fifty one are in Churchyards and the rest are in local parks scattered round the Peak District." "Good work you two, now I know we have chestnut trees, how many have been investigated by uniform?" "Just

## The Poet And The Calling Card

the ones in the woodland and they turned up nothing." "Right get behind this DI Smarty, I want results and fast. We are playing with a girl's life here. If we need overtime, I will sanction it." "Ok Ma'am." "Any ideas on the poem? Yes, Sergeant Milton?" "What if the victim's name is Chestnut and it's not a tree we are looking for?" "Not helpful Milton, unless of course you have something to change my mind." Carl was annoyed at DCI Fringe's attempt at putting him down in front of his colleagues.

"Actually Ma'am three weeks, ago a girl left her home in Ackbourne and she hasn't been seen since. Her name was Annabelle Leaf." "Sorry Milton am I missing something?" "Well the poem said A and N and she was called Annabelle and her surname is Leaf, so perhaps tree leaf?". One or two sniggered in the room. Milton ploughed on with is theory. "I think it's worth talking to her parents Ma'am" "If

## The Poet And The Calling Card

you feel it will help but I'm not holding my breath, don't waste too much time on this Milton." "Ok Ma'am." "Well unless we have anything else let's get out there and find this poor girl." "Carl?" said Gammon, "Yes Sir." "Good police work, I will come with you to Ackbourne, it's well worth a look. Let's go first thing tomorrow." "Ok Sir." John grabbed his coat and left for the night.

He knew that he should really see Sandra but the baby thing was scaring him and he just didn't know what to say to her. He knew she wanted support and for John to say he would settle down and play happy families, but he knew he wasn't ready for that. John headed for the Tow'd Man. He entered the bar area only just remembering to duck under the old beam in the entrance.

"Blimey Mr Gammon, you here again." "Just pull me a pint Angelina." Angelina smiled at John she knew the real reason he

## The Poet And The Calling Card

was at the Tow'd man. "Is Saron about?" "No John, she has gone to see the new James Bond movie." "Oh with her Mum?" "No with Matt Spanker." "Matt Spanker, he's married isn't he?" "Not anymore, apparently he and Saron have been friends for years." John knew he had no right to be annoyed but he couldn't help himself. "Are you doing food tonight?" "No because Saron is having the night off. I could make you a cheese or ham cob if you wanted John?" "No you're ok, I will nip to Up The Steps Maggie's, they do a really nice Beef Stroganoff and I fancy something hot, but thanks."

Angelina seemed a bit put out by John's rebuke, so she went to the top end of the bar to speak with some Bed and Breakfast guests. John finished his drink and left. 'What the hell is Saron playing?' at he thought.

John arrived at Up the Step's Maggie's. The bar was quite full with early door's

## The Poet And The Calling Card

drinkers and people out for an evening meal. John felt a tap on his shoulder. "Hey Sheba, how are you?" "I'm good John thanks, it seems ages since I last saw you, are you becoming a recluse?" "No just had work to do on my cottage." "Bad news about that Poet guy isn't it?" John's ear's pricked up. "What's that Sheba?" "You must know, this guy called the Poet has killed one girl and I heard you rescued one, but there is a third buried somewhere. It's been all over the six o clock news John."

John felt anger, not with Sheba, but somehow this had got out. "Will you excuse me a minute Sheba? I need to make a call?" "Sure John, I will get you a pint." "Thank you." John called Donna. "Donna have you seen the six o clock news." "Yes John, I was the one who alerted the media." "Why would you do that?" "We need help John, this girl has less than two weeks to live and if it means some old guy

# The Poet And The Calling Card

out with his dog finding the disturbed ground, then we might get a chance to save her." "That is a mistake Donna, you have opened us up to copycats now." "I'm not arguing John, I am leading this investigation and I will do it my way." "Well it would have been nice to be consulted." "Normally I would have John, but I knew you would kick off like this. Anyway I am going I have things to do see you tomorrow John" and the phone went dead. 'Damned that women' he thought.

John wandered back into the bar. The beautiful Sheba had got him a drink. "There you go John, I got you a Treacle Decale, it's a Yorkshire brew. Sorry if I ruined your night, I heard you are having it rough with the demotion and all that." "I'm ok Sheba, just used to running things my way and now I have a boss to answer to. Anyway what you doing out tonight?" "Got in from work and my flippin' cooker is playing up. so came up here for some

## The Poet And The Calling Card

dinner." "Would you like to join me?" "Love to John." Said the lovely Sheba.

"Excuse me, do you have a table for two?" "I can sit you in the Lead Miners room near the balcony overlooking Monkdale?" "Wow that would be fabulous." "Take these menus with you and I will get somebody over to take your order shortly." "Thank you." "Wow John, it must be because you are famous, no one ever get to sit there normally." "It has it's advantageous" he replied and then chuckled. Although it was dark, the full moon lit up Monkdale, it certainly was a sight to behold.

"Good evening Sir and Madam, I am Becky and I am your waitress for your dining experience tonight. We don't do a specials board, all the dishes are cooked fresh and are on our extensive menu." "I just want a main Sheba, what about you?" "Oh yes definitely John."

## The Poet And The Calling Card

"I'll have the duck in an orange jous, with parsnip truffle cakes and baby potatoes with asparagus please." "For you Madam?" "I'm spoilt for choice. I'll have the split steak, Maggie style potatoes with a hint of rosemary and the strip buttered carrots and cauliflower cheese please." "Ok thank you, would you like any wine?" "it's up to you John. Shall we have a chewy red?" "Ok by me. Could we have the Minton Merlot please?" "Certainly Sir." The waitress scurried away. "Why do you say chewy John?" "Because when it's full bodied red, it's a saying we used to have in London."

"How long were you in London?" "Oh, a hell of a long time." "What made you come back to the Peak District?" asked Sheba. "Well initially I was only here to help out on a serial killer case. My family are from near Elton well Hittington Dale to be precise. My marriage was crumbling, so it gave me a good excuse to get out.

# The Poet And The Calling Card

Then family matters took over and I'm still here." What was your wife's name?" "Lindsay" "Are you divorced?" "Yes, a long time ago, Sheba." "You don't seem to me like the marrying type or the children type of guy, John". John's mind flashed back to Sandra and the baby. Here he was again being un-faithful, well that's how it felt.

The waitress returned with the meals. "Wow, that looks fantastic and look at yours John." The waitress also had the wine and she asked if they wanted to taste it before she poured. "No that will be fine, just leave the bottle." "Oh blimey John, this Maggie's split steak is fantastic." "What is it, exactly?" "Well they split the steak, then add a mushroom, horseradish sauce with blackcurrants filling in the middle and then they bake it wrapped in streaky bacon. Heavy on the calories I bet but I will work it off." "You have got a cracking figure anyway I wouldn't worry."

# The Poet And The Calling Card

"Well that is nice of you to say John. How's the duck?" "Excellent." "So who are you seeing these days? I saw Sandra the other day, has she put a bit of weight on?" "Not sure, not seen a lot of her lately, only at work." "Oh, so are you not seeing her then? The rumour was that you had left Saron for Sandra. I can't keep up Gammon" and she laughed.

John thought at some point he is going to have to make a decision about the baby, either Sandra tells everyone she is carrying his baby or he has nothing to do with the child they were his choices.

"This meal is excellent, I best tell Kev at the Spinning Jenny that they must have a good chef here."

The night ended with John giving Sheba a peck on the cheek, nothing more, and wished her goodnight. As he got in his car he felt quite pleased with himself, but he knew by Christmas Sandra would be

## The Poet And The Calling Card

showing and he had to decide what he wanted.

John headed for home and the sanity of a quick Jameson's before bed. John lay in bed with the curtains open, all the night sky was carpeted with stars twinkling like fairy lights. He knew he had to be straight with Sandra. He had to be true to himself and he didn't want to settle down and play happy families. 'Tomorrow I will tell her' he thought.

The following morning in the cold light of day he rang Sandra. "Hey John, you ok?" "Yeah, well not really, can you call at mine on your way to work please?" "Yes of course, what's the matter?" "I will tell you when you get here?" "Ok I will be about ten minutes."

John's thoughts were everywhere. Deep down he wanted a family, now that he had lost all of his, but he knew he wasn't in love with Sandra. John's life, since the

# The Poet And The Calling Card

split from Lindsay, was about having a goodtime. The door latch went it was Sandra. She walked over to John to hold him. John politely declined the contact.

"Sandra sit down" "I don't like the sound of this John, you are worrying me" "I have given this a lot of thought and I know you will hate me for this but I am sure in the long run it will be better this way. Sandra I don't want to settle down and I don't want a baby not with you or anyone. There I have said it now."

Sandra burst into tears. "John I knew deep down this wasn't for you and I am sorry I got us in this predicament but I want this baby so that Rosie isn't an only child" "Sandra I understand and I will support you financially, anything the baby needs I will pay for."

"Do you want contact John?" "I don't think it would be a good idea for you or the child. I am sorry if this sounds callous

## The Poet And The Calling Card

but that is my decision" sighed John. "I won't tell anyone you are the father, you have had enough shit at work already, but I hope we can still be friends" John hugged Sandra and thanked her for her understanding. Sandra left for work. John finished a few jobs then he also left for Bixton.

Sergeant Milton was waiting for Gammon. "Are you ready to Ackbourne to see Mr and Mrs Leaf, Sir?" "Yes let's go and see what we can find."

Milton drove down the valley through Pritwich and on to a new build estate. "What's the address Carl?" "3 Booth Way Sir" "Well this is Booth Way. There you go, there's number three" pointed out Carl.

It was a four bed-roomed detached house with well-kept gardens. They knocked on the white PVC door. A small man came to the door, they showed him their identification.

# The Poet And The Calling Card

"What do you want?" "Mr Leaf?" "Not again! Bloody hell I'm sick of this. Henry Leaf lives at Number three Chestnut Drive just off here as you came in. I wish I had a bloody penny for every time I have had to redirect folks to his house" "Very sorry to have troubled you Sir". Milton spun the car round and they headed into the cul-de-sac on Chestnut Drive. "Chestnut? I think we may be onto something Carl" Carl beamed to think DI Gammon was impressed with him.

They knocked on the door of the neat bungalow. "Good Morning Sir, DI Gammon and Sergeant Milton, Bixton Police, I wondered if we could discuss your concern about your daughter's whereabouts?" "Certainly, come in, this is my wife Freda and I'm Henry Leaf. Tea, gentleman?" "No, we are fine, but thank you for offering". Milton sat thinking he would have liked a cup of tea.

## The Poet And The Calling Card

"You have reported your daughter missing Mr Leaf." "Please call me Henry." "Ok Henry." "Yes it was about a week ago now. Our Annabelle is a lovely girl. She goes to Church every Sunday and helps with the Sunday school." "Where does she work, Mr Leaf, sorry Henry?" "She works for Children in Need in Ackbourne she is an accountant." "Are you aware of any boyfriends?" Henry looked at his wife. His wife looked down. "I am afraid our daughter doesn't like men." John could sense the discomfort in Henry's voice. "Sorry to probe, but this is important, are you saying Annabelle is a lesbian?" Henry nodded "Yes."

"Ok well not a problem Henry, we are not here to talk about Annabelle's preferences just anything that may be relevant to her not returning home. Can you run through when she didn't come home?" "Ok Mr Gammon, Annie, that's what we called her at home. Annie is a sweet girl she did well

## The Poet And The Calling Card

at school always went to Church, never misses, she has been all over the world with the Church. She told us, when we were ribbing her about a boy from Church who had asked her out one time, it was then that she told us she was gay. To be honest I wasn't shocked and I don't disapprove. To my knowledge she only has ever been out with one girl and they have been together for almost four years."
"What is her name and address Henry?"
"Her name is Rachel Fiche. She works in the office with our Annie. She has her own place in Ackbourne Cotton Mill, you know the one's they converted about five year back."

"I think our Annie would have moved in with her but I need so much help with Freda, her mum, she has Alzheimer's and to be honest with you, I needed the rest from it, she is a good girl she spends hours with her Mum."

## The Poet And The Calling Card

"Ok so other than the Church, incidentally which Church did she attend?" "Pritwich Mr Gammon, reverend Matthew Spouncer is a great vicar, he has been at Pritwich for five years and has done so much for local charities. Her life was the Church, looking after her Mum and spending time with Rachel. Have you got a lead on her Mr Gammon?" "No not at the moment but I am sure she will have her reasons, she is twenty four so she will know her own mind. Kid's hey Henry?" Gammon and Milton got up to leave. "You will find our daughter Mr Gammon won't you?" "We will do our best Henry as long as she wants to be found."

Gammon and Milton got in the car. "Chestnut Drive. Carl my gut feeling is you are correct. This is the girl but where has he got her that's the question?"

Gammon and Milton arrived back at Bixton. Gammon was met by DCI Fringe. "John, do you have a minute?" "Yes

# The Poet And The Calling Card

Ma'am." Fringe took John into a side room. "You have just received another Orange envelope. I would like to roll this out to the media John and I know you were not happy last time but we have to see the media in these cases as our friend, not the enemy."

John smiled, 'That's naive in the extreme degree' he thought. "Look Donna, you are running the show it's your call, just a word of caution from my perspective. We don't want copy-cat's or amateur detectives trying to find these victims. Before you go in front of the media, I think the initial thought that this victim is buried under a Chestnut tree, is wrong. I have just been with Milton and I believe Annabelle Leaf is our third victim. She disappeared recently and she lives on Chestnut Drive. Let's see what's in the orange envelope."

"Hello Mr Gammon,

# The Poet And The Calling Card

Can I say I am sorry you have been demoted and I hope that it is nothing to do with me? I find it quite funny that your new DCI as got all the plods searching all the chestnut trees in the Peak District. I have been watching you and I will be fair. You and that Sergeant of yours are right, Annabelle Leaf is my victim so well done you two. Now for the clue as to where she is buried"

*Look up Look down and round and round*
*Feeling dizzy may astound.*
*Dig deep in your soul and you will find the girl you crave to find.*

*By day and night I'm not alone*
*The thoughts I think are not my own*
*So dig deep my friend for all you're worth.*

# The Poet And The Calling Card

*My grave you will find in a wood that was once the hunting ground of the king but now it's just for walking dogs*
**Please find me somebody**
**The Poet."**

"What do you make of that John?" "I know where she is Donna. Kings Wood in Elton let's get every available man down there."

Every available officer was sent to Kings Wood, Elton armed with shovels. Kings Wood was some twenty seven acres in size and was once the hunting ground of the Kings of England, when it was part of Sherwood Forest. For some reason and historians don't know why but Kings Wood had an abundance of deer and other species to hunt.

Gammon stayed through the night until the early hours of the following day. DI Warren Cus'tard took over with DI Lee.

## The Poet And The Calling Card

Call me immediately we find something. The victim could be anywhere but my feeling is it will be by a tree for a marker so look for disturbed ground. "Will do Sir, get off and get some sleep." Gammon phoned Donna. "Donna don't use the media yet, I don't want Mr and Mrs Leaf having big expectations, we only have a slim chance of finding this girl alive." "Agree John, get off and get some sleep." "I will just have a couple of hours and I will be back." said John

As John drove back to the cottage, he had been on duty for almost twenty six hours and was feeling shattered. He climbed the stairs and just flopped on the bed, within a few minutes he was sound asleep.

John woke again just as it was going dark, he looked at the time on his phone it was 4.48pm he shot out of bed and still with the same clothes on he drove back to Kings Wood. When he arrived the officers

## The Poet And The Calling Card

were leaving. "What's happening?" "We have covered most of the wood, all we found was some flowers on a dog's grave about halfway in John."

"Show me" he retorted to DI Cus'tard. Cus'tard, who looked annoyed he was tired and it had been a long day. They walked in silence to the spot of the dog's grave. "There you go John satisfied? Right I'm off I am bloody knackered." John felt annoyed, some poor girl was fighting for her life and this is the level of commitment Bixton officers had. He then re-phrased that in his mind as Cus'tard wasn't from Bixton.

The dog grave had a small cross on it with the dog's name "REX". Fresh flowers were on the grave so somebody still cared. Where the hell was it. He was just about to leave and with only the torch on his phone for light, something told him to look behind the tree. From the back of the tree

# The Poet And The Calling Card

he could see there had been some kind of trench had been filled in. Gammon followed it. At the next tree John could see the pipe. 'She is here' he thought. He quickly rung DCI Fringe and told her what he had found, then frantically started to dig with his bare hands, being careful not to disturb the air pipe.

It was a pretty hopeless task, the team were soon back and with large lighting and several more men. They started to dig, Gammon reiterated about the pipe. "You ok John? You look dreadful." "I will be if this poor girl is alive and well in her grave Donna."

After almost half an hour of digging, they finally found the girl. "Ma'am" one of the uniformed lads shouted "You better see this" Fringe and Gammon ran over. Fringe was immediately sick by the sight that met her. The poor girls head was in the grave, she had been decapitated. Gammon

## The Poet And The Calling Card

slumped against the nearest tree. If only he hadn't gone home to sleep maybe they could have saved her.

The area was sealed off and the Forensic boys were left to do their job. Gammon and Fringe went back to Bixton to break the news to the rest of the officers. "Once we know for sure that it is Annabelle Leaf, I will inform the parents. I don't want any leaks to the press on this, we need to be sure we have the right person. We will have a meeting in the Incident room at 9.00am tomorrow when forensics will be able to tell us the facts. Everyone needs to be there please." Gammon drove home feeling despair in his heart.
That poor girl and her family, how was Henry going to cope now?

John showered and did what he always did when he was feeling worthless, that was find a pub and get hammered. He knew

## The Poet And The Calling Card

this wasn't the right thing to do but that's how he coped with the traumas of the job.

As John left the cottage Roger Glazeback was swilling out the milking parlour. "Hey John, glad I have seen you. There was a bloke knocking on your door this morning, said his name was Saul Horobin. He gave me this number to pass onto you." "Ok, thanks Roger, I know who it is, I will call him."

John called Horobin's number. The gravelly voice of Saul Horobin answered. "Saul?, John Gammon here." "Oh hi John, I tried to contact you yesterday, would you believe I dropped my bloody phone with all my contacts in a river in France?" "Yes I would believe Saul, you have always been a clumsy buggar. What have you got for me?" "Quite a bit actually, can we meet up?" "Where are you now?" "I am at a pub called the Spinning Jenny in a village called Swinster, do you know it

## The Poet And The Calling Card

John?" "Yes, order me a pint of Pedigree and I will be with you in ten minutes Saul." "Ok John, but you know it will be on your bill as expenses" and Saul laughed.

John arrived at the Spinning Jenny and Kev pointed John in the direction of Saul. Saul Horobin was about five foot eight and maybe nine stone wet through. He had a large mole just below his right eye. 'He wasn't at the front of the queue when they were handing out looks' John thought.

Saul stood up to shake hands with John. "Good to see you again John." "Likewise, Saul." "How have you ended up here, never thought your Lindsay would ever leave London?" "We split up ages ago, divorced now Saul, I think she is back down London. I got the opportunity to help on a murder case in the Peak District, where I was born and raised, so it was a good opportunity to get away. Cut a long

# The Poet And The Calling Card

story short ended up staying here and work out of Bixton Station. Anyway what you got for me." "Quite a lot John, the lady in question" and Saul pushed a picture of her across the table. She was the spitting image of John. She had long black hair, piercing blue eyes and about five feet ten tall.

"What's her name Saul? "Fleur Fournier. Although she recently divorced, and reverted back to her maiden name, which was Dubois. Fleur Dubois, as she is now, lives in Colmar. She is an interpreter for Beloise Banking Group. She travels a lot, they have sites all over the globe. She was married to Sacha Fournier two years ago. He had an affair with his secretary, which ended the marriage. They never had children and had been married four years."

"Saul you are a magician." "Here are the rest of the pictures I took and her address in Colmar. The only thing I would say is

## The Poet And The Calling Card

she does travel, so it will be pot luck if you decide to go to Colmar to see her John." "Saul can't thank you enough, send me your bill and I will settle it straight away."
Saul finished his drink and said that now John was happy, he was going to check out and get back to London tonight. He left John feeling in a much better place than when he first walked in.

"Looking pleased John." John told Kev the story and showed him the pictures, he knew he could trust Kev. "Bloody hell she is like you and Graham lad." "Uncanny, hey Kev?" "So what now then?" "Not sure, my heart tells me to get the next flight to Colmar, but my head say's think it through. What do you think?" "Well if it was me, I would think it through. There are a lot of ramifications here John, she may not know she was adopted, then you have Maggie Else to consider and not being spiteful or protective here, she could

## The Poet And The Calling Card

contest what Graham left you." "I'm not bothered about that Kev." "You say that now lad, but you don't know her do you?" "Yeah, you are right, best sleep on it."

"Hey John how are you?" "Good Cheryl, you three been to badminton I see." Sheba smiled and Doreen growled "Bloody lost again, I am sure Sheba cheats." "Oh it won't have anything to do with your dodgy hip and Cheryl's dodgy knee then?" "Shut up and get us a drink." "Right what you having?" "I'll have a pint of lager shandy please John." "Cheryl?" "Same for me please" "And for you Sheba?" "Brandy and coke please." "Double?" "Why not Mr Gammon."

"So, are you all set for Barcelona on Friday?" John winced, he had forgotten to book time off with everything going on at work. "I hear you will be fighting them off John. Joni and Jo's sister, Tracey, are going on their own!!!"

# The Poet And The Calling Card

John smiled at Sheba, then saw his chance "I hear you have a new fella you are taking?" "I have known Paul forever, he used to help on the farm." "It's Paul Dirk isn't it Sheba?" "Yeah do you know him Cheryl?" "Isn't he a fitter up at Barley's Fabrication at Lingcliffe?" "That's the one Cheryl." "Don't know him very well but I think Bob played cricket with him a few years back. He loves his cricket almost made it for Yorkshire but he broke his middle finger in a motorbike accident and could never bowl the same at that level."

"What time do we leave on Friday?" "Bus takes us to East Midlands Airport at 7.00am and we fly at 10.15am John." "Looking forward to it." "Bet you are, with those two beauties hanging on your every word. hey Doreen?" "He is bloody debauched" and they all laughed. Just then John's phone rang. "Excuse me ladies, I need to take this." "It will be one of the

## The Poet And The Calling Card

harem I'll bet." John just smiled at Doreen and wandered over to a quiet corner.

"John, Saul here, I forgot to mention she has a criminal record." "What?said John. "Yeah she was guilty of tax evasion three years ago and looking at the case files it wasn't so much her, her husband's accountant filed the wrong figures, but she was implicated. She got three months suspended John." "Ok, thanks Saul."

John returned to the girls and Kev, who by now were in top voice. "Are you having a single room John?" "No he isn't, the hotel only has double rooms." "That was lucky then, John." "Right you lot, you win, I am having a quick drink in the Tow'd Man before bedtime." "Cuddles with Saron?", they shouted as he left.

John arrived at the Tow'd Man mindful of what he had to do tomorrow. The worst

## The Poet And The Calling Card

part of the job, was having to tell a family they had lost a loved one.

"Hi John, surprised to see you." "Just called for a quick one before going home. You on your own?", he replied "Angelina's just gone up, she was on breakfasts this morning."

"So, it's nice to see you. How's it going at work?" John told Saron what he had to do tomorrow, he trusted her, she knew how these things worked. "Not a nice job John. If you are true to form you need a double brandy am I correct?" "Spot on Saron, are you joining me?" "Can't see us getting any busier tonight once those two couples have left, so why not."

"I see you donated a lot of money to Dilley Dale Hospital, it's lovely that they renamed it after Annie. Mum was so pleased John. She is always asking me if I am seeing you. You know what Mum is like." "She is lovely Saron." All the time

# The Poet And The Calling Card

John was looking at Saron, he had butterflies in his tummy, he knew deep down she was the one but could not bring himself to commit.

Four double brandies later the pub had emptied and Saron had come round to sit with John. They chatted for a further two hours with lots of Brandy flowing.

"John, am I reading something into you being here tonight?" "What do mean?" "I think you know what I mean, about us?" "Saron you are the complete package but since Lindsay I can't commit and I know you need that and I understand that." "John, I'm not going to shackle you and at some point you have to get over Lindsay and learn to trust again." "It would be no good me promising something I can't do Saron. Look perhaps I should go." "John stay and hold me tonight I want you by my side." "If you want me to stay, I will of course." "I just want to be cuddled John." "I understand."

# The Poet And The Calling Card

They left the bar and retired to Saron's bedroom. They both undressed and Saron commented that she was leaving her underwear on so she wasn't tempted. John smiled but he completely stripped off. They climbed into bed and Saron cuddled John, she rested her head on his chest and put her arms tightly round him. "Do you know John, I never fancied a man with a hairy chest, until we got together." "Lucky for me then hey?" and he laughed. They lay talking for almost an hour but as John expected their lust or was it love got the better of them and they made passionate love. After their love making Saron had a little cry. John was a bit lost on what to do.

"I'm sorry John, I'm just being silly I was thinking this time last year we had a lovely Christmas together. Will you come for Christmas dinner this year to Mum's?" "Look I'm not being awkward just not sure what I am doing. I have something to tell you?" "Not sure I like the sound of

## The Poet And The Calling Card

this John." "My Uncle Graham, who was my real father, had another child. I had a private detective find her, she was brought up in France, she was adopted there." "Who was her mother?" "I promised I would not say Saron." "Not your Mum?" "No nothing like that. Anyway I have tracked her down and I am going to try and contact her." "Do you think that's wise John?" "Saron, she is all the family I have and if she knocks me back, she does, but I am going to try."

"Best let you get some sleep after our lovemaking Mr Gammon." "Perhaps a good idea" he said and he kissed Saron.

The following morning John woke to the smell of bacon, Saron was downstairs cooking, so he showered and dressed and went down. "Only done you bacon sandwiches, is that ok?" "That's lovely Saron." Out of the blue she flung her arms round him. "I love you Mr Gammon."

# The Poet And The Calling Card

John would not commit, "You know what I think of you" he said.

John finished his sandwiches and coffee and gave Saron a kiss. "When will I see you again John?" "I'll call you, bye." John left quickly trying to avoid the commitment. John headed for the station, Bill Bixall on radio Ackbourne had just done the weather. Heavy snow given for parts of the Peak District. It was a good job John had garaged the Jag for the Freelander if the weather was going to be bad.

By the time he had taken his coat off and grabbed a coffee, everyone was assembled in the incident room. DCI Fringe strode in purposefully. "Ok let us start off with yesterday's victim that DI Gammon almost saved. John?" Wally got up. "The victim was female and by dental records her name was." John held his breath. "Annabelle Leaf. Ma'am, I believe we already know the address of where she

## The Poet And The Calling Card

lived. Sadly Annabelle's head was severed at some point as the ground was being filled in. She must have either moved forward and the wire garrotted her. I don't think the murderer knew. We have no DNA, this person knows what they are doing." "Thank you." John Walvin sat back down.

"Ok we have nothing to chase up on here, where are we on connections? Do we see anything? The second victim who survived, Michelle Wilkinson, went to Church regularly, as did the third victim Annabelle Leaf. There is no connection on the first victim Mandy Nichol." "Ok John and DI Jeanine Fairfield will speak with Mr and Mrs Leaf, DI Cus'tard and DI Lee, let's try a bit harder to get a lead on these envelopes the killer is using. Scooper and Milton let's find out if Victims two and three knew each other through their Church activities. DI Smarty, have we any news on Chan Chi? I want this bastard

## The Poet And The Calling Card

catching." "Nothing new Ma'am, it's like he just disappeared." "Well I'm not happy with your answer, so get digging and find this maniac."

"Before we all go, the station Christmas Piss Up is at the Tow'd Man this year, let's try and have a decent turn out hey? Let's go everyone."

"She is a bit full on isn't she John?" "Yeah a bit, Dave. Give her a chance, she is trying to make her mark. Good luck with Chi." "I need a bloody miracle, not good luck John, see you later."

"Are you ready Jeanine?" "Ready when you are." Fairfield and Gammon headed for Henry Leafs home and the tragic news he had to give him and his poor wife.

Henry met them at the door. "Lovely to see you again Mr Gammon, have you some good news for me? Do you know it's unbelievable, I dreamt you would find her

# The Poet And The Calling Card

safe and sound come in come in." "Henry, please sit down. Where is your wife?" "She isn't good today Mr Gammon, she doesn't recognise me and she keeps shouting at me to get out of her house." "Oh I am sorry Mr Leaf. This is my colleague DI Jeanine Fairfield. I am afraid we have bad news for you."

John could sense the despair in Henry Leaf's face. "We found your daughter, but I am afraid she was murdered." "No, No," Henry wailed. Jeanine put her arms round him. "We are so sorry Mr Leaf." "How did she die?" "Henry I am not sure this is the right time." "I need to know Mr Gammon." By now Henry's right arm was visibly shaking, John hadn't noticed it before and he wondered if he had the start of on-set Parkinson's disease.

"Are you ok Henry?" "Yes Mr Gammon, but I want to know" "It appears the murderer was burying her alive and he had secured any movement with very sharp

## The Poet And The Calling Card

wire like piano wire round her neck and we think as her grave was being filled the weight of the soil made her move her head and it decapitated her. I am so sorry Henry." "Why would somebody do this to my beautiful daughter?" "I have to ask you to come to the station to formally identify Annabelle's body. We can arrange a car for you and for a liaison office to sit with your wife. Would you like some counselling Henry?". Henry shook his head and indicated he didn't. "Have you anybody who can sit with you?" Again Henry just shook his head indicating he didn't have. "DI Fairfield will sit with you today Henry, then tomorrow she will sit with your wife while you identify the body. Is that ok?" Hardly able to speak Henry said thank you.

"A word please, Jeanine." Henry sat in the chintz flowered chair looking out of the window onto his beautifully tended garden, his whole world shattered. "Are

# The Poet And The Calling Card

you ok to sit with Henry? I think he is in a bit of shock" "Well I guess he would be John." "Arrange things for tomorrow with Sergeant Yap please. I am going to have a chat with Annabelle's friend.2

John shook hands with Henry and offered him and his wife his condolences he then left.

The ride to Ackbourne to the Children In Need offices, was full of black thoughts for John. 'What a cruel world we live in' he thought. He had just turned the Leaf family's world upside down and for what? So some maniac with some kind of illness could laugh about it? Gammon arrived at the charity building, an old Victorian building, a former work house which was a bit ironic Gammon thought.

Gammon showed his identification to the receptionist. "Could I speak with Rachel Fiche please?" "Just a moment Mr Gammon, I will try her extension."

# The Poet And The Calling Card

"Rachel? I have a Detective Inspector Gammon in reception for you." "She will be down in a minute Mr Gammon."

"Rachel Fiche?" "Yes, how can I help you?" "Have you a room we can talk privately?" "I'm just going into the conference room with Mr Gammon Jenny." "Ok." said the receptionist. Rachel took John into a plush oak panelled conference room. "What is this about Mr Gammon?" "Did you know Annabelle Leaf, Miss Fiche?" "Please call me Rachel." "Ok Rachel." "Yes we worked together." "When was the last time you saw Annabelle?" "Is this about her disappearance?" "Just answer the question please Rachel." "Your tone, Mr Gammon, sounds more like I am being investigated, do I need a solicitor?" "That is up to you, we can do this formally at the station or as we are now Rachel, your choice?" "I saw Annabelle about two weeks ago we had a drink after work at the Prosecco bar in

## The Poet And The Calling Card

town." "Is that something you did regularly?" "Sometimes, not often, if we had to work late we would sometimes have an evening meal after work." "Were you in a relationship with Annabelle?" For the first time Fiche lost the air of confidence she was portraying previously. "What is this about? the girl hasn't been to work for almost two weeks what's going on?" "Answer the question please Rachel?" "Yes we had a fling, nothing more", she said. "A four year fling, perhaps?" "Look it was more off than on. Annabelle wasn't sure if she was gay, if that's what you want to hear."

"So you had an on off relationship with a girl you worked with, when exactly was the last time you saw Annabelle?" "A couple of weeks back, it was a Friday we worked until about 6.40pm so I assumed we would go out, but she said she was going home and getting a take away for her bloody parents. Can you believe?" "So

## The Poet And The Calling Card

did you argue?" "To be honest, yes we did. I mean, I have had four years of this and she was so goody two shoes with her Church work and her bloody parents. She was always having to check things before she could do the things I wanted to do."

Gammon could see this was an aggressive woman. "So after you argued, where did you leave her?" "She walked across town and I drove off. I told her she could go to hell I wasn't having a relationship with her parents, I wanted it with her." "What did Annabelle say?" "Like she always said, hardly anything, she wouldn't argue she said it was bad for the soul."

"Miss Fiche, I am sorry to tell you that Annabelle Leaf was found dead yesterday, she had been murdered" Fiche looked shocked. "Can I go now?" "Yes you may, but I may need to speak with you again." Rachel Fiche walked out. 'What a hardnosed cow' John thought.

## The Poet And The Calling Card

On the way back to the station Gammon informed DCI Fringe of his conversation with Rachel Fiche. "Can you run a background check on her? There is something I don't like about her Donna" "Ok John see you in a short while."

Gammon arrived back at the station and as soon as he saw Donna he realised he hadn't said he was on holiday tomorrow. "Donna before I forget, I am off tomorrow, going to Barcelona for a couple of nights" Donna's face went very stern. "I like my officers to at least give me a months' notice John. The workload we have and the situation with this killer, who seems hell bent on communicating just through you for some reason, leaves the situation a bit poor but if you have booked it, then I suppose there is little else I can say on the subject but in future I require more notice."

John thought "well that's me told". Sergeant Yap stood grinning behind

# The Poet And The Calling Card

Donna's back. "Ok, did you run the background checks?" "Yes come to my office." DCI Fringe ordered two coffees then she informed Gammon of her findings. "Your gut feeling seems to be correct John, our Miss Fiche appears to have a temper. She is originally from Hull and has moved about a bit. When she was nineteen she spent three months in prison for attacking a girl in a nightclub with a broken glass. Guess what? it appears the girl was her lover and she was chatting to some guy she had been in school with and Miss Jealous Pants threw a wobbly. After leaving HM Prison Hull she next turns up in Stoke-on-Trent, living with a Sonia Blake, a lady quite a few years older than her. Police were called to Mrs Blake's house as our Miss Fiche was threatening Sonia Blake with a carving knife. Apparently Mrs Blake had split with her husband over an affair with Fiche, but after three months had decided she was batting for the other side and told Fiche

# The Poet And The Calling Card

she was going back to her husband. Fiche could not handle it and kicked off big style. She got two and half years for that and was released five years ago from HMS Werrington Prison, Stoke on Trent, since then nothing, until this connection today." "Bloody hell, this is interesting. Isn't Werrington a young offender's institute?" "Correct John, it doesn't say why they put her there in the report. I am trying to get a psychiatric report from her time in prison."

"Look Donna, I will be back on Monday, if we can get the psychiatric reports for Fiche and a warrant to search her property, that would be good." "Yes will sort that John." "Oh and let's say she comes to the station at 11.00am with her solicitor, that will give us a bit of time in case anything turns up over the weekend." "Yes good Idea." "You better get off, enjoy your weekend in Barcelona John." "Thanks Donna and I am sorry for not telling you

## The Poet And The Calling Card

sooner." "Sure you have had a fair bit on your mind, have a good one."

John left the station thinking to himself how Donna was correct, it was a bit selfish with everything going off. On his way back home he called at the Spinning Jenny to sort arrangements out for the Barcelona trip. The gang were already having a drink. As he walked in the bar he could hear Doreen chastising Kev. "Only taking a crate to have on the way to the airport, my lovely." "Well make sure it is only one, it's not a bloody booze up. I want to see some of the lovely architecture." "I agree Doreen, so you better be listening Bob." "You tell him Cheryl." "Waste of time me telling Jack, he will do his own thing anyway." "You can always try Shelley." "I have been trying for thirty years Jo, I think I have lost that one." Jack sat smiling to himself. John ordered a round. Tracey Rodgers gave him a hand with the drinks.

# The Poet And The Calling Card

"Right listen up everybody, we fly at 7.10am in the morning from East Midlands Airport. The mini bus will be leaving the Spinning Jenny at 4.30am. If you are not here we can't wait, we will have to go." Everyone nodded in agreement.

"Our hotel is the Barceló Royal, it's a half mile walk to the centre so perfectly placed to see Barcelona. We have a trip on Saturday night to the Guarida family vineyard for a Tapas and VIP wine tasting experience. Sunday I have booked all the men on the guided tour of Barcelona FC and I thought we girls could go shopping." Big cheer went up. "We arrive back Monday morning at 10.30am at East Midlands and a mini bus will bring us back to the Spinning Jenny. Any questions anybody?"

"Steve?" "Yeah if my sister-in-law doesn't like sleeping on her own could our Policeman stud help out?" Jo gave Steve

## The Poet And The Calling Card

the biggest dig in the ribs. His comment went down like a lead balloon. "I'm only joking Tracey, oh and John." "Stick to Bob telling the jokes, Steve." "Think I best Kev."

By 9.30pm everyone had gone home, so John left too. Arriving home he packed his bags and went straight to bed.

John's alarm went off at 3.30am he showered shaved then headed for the Spinning Jenny. When John arrived he was second to last on the bus with no sign of Bob and Cheryl. "Have you tried ringing them Doreen?" "Look Kev, I made it quite clear 4.30am and we were leaving. It's now 4.30am so we are." The bus set off without Bob and Cheryl. The journey took about forty five minutes. As they queued up for the tickets a red face Bob appeared. "Where have you been?" "Had a bloody flat tyre coming up Lingcliffe and I didn't have a jack in the car because I always call the AA but there was no

## The Poet And The Calling Card

signal. Cheryl tried to call, but she couldn't get through. Anyway just by luck one of the Maintenance fitters at Pippa's Frozen Foods was going on shift, so he sorted it for me. Cheryl is parking the car now."

Cheryl arrived not looking in the least bit pleased. "Hey come on, you are here now, so let's have a good time." "I know Shelly, I just could not believe we didn't have a Jack in the car" and she glared at Bob. "Come on we have the tickets, let's get through security then we can have a drink." "Blimey your mates like a beer Jo." "You ain't seen nothing yet Tracey."

By the time they had landed in Barcelona, gone through customs, picked up their luggage and transferred to the hotel, it was 12.10pm. John was pleased with his room, it even had a hot tub. They had decided to have a wander round Barcelona and have a few drinks then a meal. First up was a

## The Poet And The Calling Card

small back street bar the type the locals would drink at.

"Four jugs of Sangria please Camarero." Steve couldn't stop laughing "Camarero? where has that come from?" "It means waiter in Spanish, Steve." "Well he doesn't look best pleased with you, did you say it right?" "Of course I did." The guy came over put down the four large jugs of Sangria then turned to Kev and said "I am the Propietario, not the waiter Sir." Kev went bright red and tried apologising, all the lads were laughing, the women were being a bit more caring.

"Guess we best have this and move on, he is none too pleased with me." The next bar they found, also down a back alley, was aptly called Barra de los locales. "This looks good." "So what does the sign say Kev, seeing how you know Spanish?" "Stop it Steve" Jo said. "Think Barra is a fish?"

# The Poet And The Calling Card

They went inside John ordered four jugs of Sangria. The bar person came over. "Is this a fish restaurant mate?" Kev said. The barman shrugged his shoulders and looked at Kev as if he was an alien. "Sorry mate I have to tell you Barra de los locales is me and Bar for the locals. No fish here Bud."

By now Bob was a bit fresh, "I can't wait to tell them back home about the fish bar Kev took us to." "I would suggest you behave yourself Mr. No Jack hey Cheryl?" "Too right Kev." Bob sat down feeling deflated. It was now almost 3.30pm. "I'm getting hungry Doreen. Shall we find somewhere to have a snack? Jo's hungry too." "Fine by me and me Shelley." "Ok let's ask this guy the best place to eat." John stood up "Dónde está el mejor lugar para comer?" "Dos puertas más abajo. Gracias, Senor." "Got that last bit John, but where did you learn to be so fluent?" "My ex-wife had this thing about learning a language so I went to night classes with

## The Poet And The Calling Card

her Tracey." "Only John Gammon would be this cool" "I agree Shelly" replied Joni.

"Come on two doors down." It turned out to be an English Bar the Dun Cow. "Maybe your Spanish isn't that good Porky and he was telling you something" and Steve laughed. "I'm not bothered, I'm starving Steve."

With all the food ordered and the lads with a pint of Bass each, everything in the garden was rosy. It's basic food but it will do to put us on until we eat later. "Are we stopping out all night?" "Might as well, no point in going back then coming out again, Cheryl." "Didn't Jackie fancy coming." "No somebody has to look after the business Jack." "That's the problem when you work for yourself Jack hey?" "Anyone up for Jack's?" "Not all afternoon Steve." "Ok just a couple of games." They laid out the cards and Steve dealt. The Dun Cow was quite well recreated and the owner

## The Poet And The Calling Card

was a cockney, so plenty of rattle John thought.

The first Jack went to Jo, Brandy. The next Jack landed with Doreen, Pernod. "Bloody hell that's going to knock somebody side-ways." Third Jack out went to Bob. "I'm ok with paying for it, hopefully I won't get to drink it." Famous last words, the fourth Jack out was again Bob. He went green as he downed it in one. They all clapped. "Next game please" shouted Steve. First Jack out went to Tracey, "What do I do?" she asked. "Just name a drink Tracey." "Ok Tequila". The next Jack out went to Shelley, Hendricks Gin, third Jack went to Jack Etchings he duly paid and the fourth Jack poor Bob got it again.

They had four more games and poor Bob got another three of the four to drink, never been known before, he had drunk five out of the six concoctions with Tracey Rodgers getting the other one. Steve had

## The Poet And The Calling Card

paid for two; John paid for one; Bob paid for one; Jack paid for one and Kev got hit for the last one. It was almost 9.30pm when they staggered out of the bar. "I'm taking Bob back, he can hardly walk." "We will help you Cheryl." "Thanks Shelley." "Yeah we have had enough haven't we Steve?" Steve didn't answer, he was just warming up. Everyone decided to go back except John and Tracey. Joni wanted to stay but could hardly play gooseberry she thought. "Don't do anything I wouldn't do Porky, she is my sister-in-law you know?" John gave Steve a one fingered salute as he left.

"Right where do you fancy going now John?" "I know of a little bar that plays music, just a guy on a piano and a woman on a double bass but it's supposed to be good." "Have you been before John?" "No I researched it on Trip Advisor."

"Does that make you clever or cunning perhaps Mr Gammon?" Tracey smiled at

## The Poet And The Calling Card

John. "Let's see at the end of the night" John replied. They arrived at John's little piano bar. The bar was in a dimly lit cellar down a metal spiral staircase. The walls were painted purple but everything else had a coat of black. Tracey turned to John "Are you sure about this John?" "It will be fine, although it's a bit different than what I envisaged." At the bar a girl of about twenty seven years old with heavy make up on, asked them what they wanted. "What would you recommend?" "I would say a Pastis 45 and a glass of Stella." "Two of them then please." The girl smiled and returned a few minutes later with the drinks. "Cheers John," "Yeah cheers Tracey. So you split from your husband?" "Well it was going to be a break but to be honest I don't want to go back down London, things haven't been right for a while and I wonder if I am trying to revive a dying plant. What about you? You said early your ex-wife who was she?" "Her name was Lindsay she was a

## The Poet And The Calling Card

Derbyshire girl, it's a long story but we got together when I took her to London" "So what happened?" "She had an affair with a pompous prick and we split again, a long story but all water under the bridge now" "Are you seeing anyone now then?" "No not really." "Come on Gammon, let's have a straight answer" "Well ok, No. Why do you ask?" "Just curiosity. Here let me get the next drink" "No way, I'm old fashioned, I buy the drinks" "Wow, a proper man, that's a first" and she laughed.

After a further four drinks and numerous Billy Joel songs, they called it a night. They walked back to the hotel. Tracey linked her arm in Johns as they walked along chatting happily. Once at the lift John decided to take his chance. "Would you like a nightcap in my room?" "No, enjoyed your company John but that's it, see you in the morning" and she got out of the lift on the second floor. 'How odd?'

## The Poet And The Calling Card

John thought, not something that happened to him very often.

The following morning at breakfast poor Bob looked dreadful. He didn't want to come down, but Cheryl had paid for his Barcelona football trip, so he had no choice. She still wasn't over the car jack incident or him getting drunk.

"Are you feeling rough mate?" "Just a bit Steve" "Here, get this down you" and Steve handed Bob a pint of Guinness. Bob went white "Thanks but I couldn't" "Try it lad, you will feel better almost straight away" "Suppose I can't feel any worse Jack." With great trepidation Bob downed the pint of Guinness in one. Bob went very quiet but after ten minutes or so he said he felt loads better. "See, a hair of the dog old lad" "You were not wrong you two" "Ok lads please look after Bob today and bloody behave, the lot of you. Have a good day and your bus is back here at 8.00pm tonight" "Go steady on that credit

## The Poet And The Calling Card

card Doreen". She glared at Kev, "Only saying my lovely". The girls all left for their shopping spree and the lads climbed on the coach taking them to the Nou Camp.

Bob sat with John. "Don't think I have ever known you this quiet Bob?" "I am never playing that game again" "Well at least you are going to a proper football ground today" "Bet it's not as good as Pride Park John". Derby's ground isn't as old as the Nou Camp. John smiled Bob would have nothing said against his beloved Derby.

It was a bright day, perfect for looking round this fabulous stadium, the tour had just finished when John's mobile rang. "Hello" "John? Donna here, I have just been called into work. Another Orange envelope has turned up addressed to you, I need to open it, John are you ok with that?" "Of course Donna, read it out to me please."

# The Poet And The Calling Card

"Ok John, here we go. *"Well my friend you found the girl again, shame she lost her head before you found her but that's the game we play. I will try to be more careful with your next victim."*

*"How can you sit and watch as she draws her last breath?"*

*"While you enjoy the sun, she is in the dark waiting to be found. It's cold, it's damp here."*

*"Now you want a clue my little Keystone cop. Try looking in a drop, its not where you think me to be so think carefully."*

*Good luck my friend Tick Tock".*

*The Poet*

"Donna, I will get a flight back, this poor girl is relying on us". "Your choice John" "I'm on my way Donna". "What's the problem John?" "There has been a

## The Poet And The Calling Card

development in the murder cases at work, I am going to have to fly back tonight." "Bloody hell, can't they wait a couple of days mate? you are allowed your holidays". John couldn't tell Steve, but two more days maybe the difference between life and death for the next victim. John asked Steve to explain to everyone and he left in a taxi, picked up his luggage and was on a plane back to the UK by 2.00pm.

John landed at East Midlands and Donna Fringe was waiting. "Sorry about this John, I feel like a right cow having argued with you before you went, then you coming back early. I wish some other people I have worked with had the same work ethic as you." "All part of the job Donna." "I have called an emergency meeting in the incident room and asked that everyone attend. We owe it to this poor girl."

# The Poet And The Calling Card

Once back at Bixton the only person missing was DI Scooper, she apparently had a tummy bug. John knew what the tummy bug was, but obviously could not say.

"Ok gather round all of you, we have received another Orange envelope addressed to DI Gammon. I'll pass it round, take a look and I am looking for constructive comments please." After a few minutes DI Cus'tard put his hand up. "They are referring to a drop, what do we think the term drop means? Is she held in a cavern where stalactites are formed from drops from the roof of the caves perhaps?" "Yes DI Lee?" "Does he mean he has dropped her off somewhere?" "Look this is going to be a long night I suggest we get Rinko Bolan back in and whilst he is here I want his place searching. Also anybody contacted his previous employers Gosberton Pickers in Lincolnshire?" "The guy who owns the company wasn't back

## The Poet And The Calling Card

until today, I have his mobile, I will call him Ma'am" "Ok Milton, get back to me urgently. John, I want you to interview Rachel Fiche with DI Lee. DI Smarty, you and DI Fairfield interview Bolan, you should have the information from Milton by the time we have him in custody. I also want her place searching. Ok we all know what we have to do, sorry for ruining your weekend but this poor girl has less than two weeks to live, let's get it sorted."

DCI Fringe pulled John aside "You are good at these poems John, take another look, will he contact you again with a name?" "Well if he is true to form he will". Gammon went to his office while the beat lads got the suspects and their solicitors in for formal interviews.

John read the poem numerous times and he kept coming back to the word drop. 'Did he mean 'drop' in the context that it was written?' he wondered.

# The Poet And The Calling Card

Finally Rinko Bolan along with his solicitor arrived at the station and were put into interview room two, whilst Rachel Fiche and her solicitor were put in interview room one.

Milton had some news from Gosberton Pickers. "Apparently Rinko Bolan had been seeing a local Gosberton woman by the name of Caroline Grace. They had been out drinking and got into a fight when they got to Grace's flat and Bolan almost murdered her. Her brother worked at Gosberton Pickers also and he got into it with Bolan, so the owner sacked Bolan. Neither of the incidents were ever reported for some reason. I have told DCI Fringe and Dave Smarty Sir" "Ok thanks Carl".

Gammon entered the interview room and DI Lee set the tape to record. "November 27th. Interview with Rachel Fiche, her solicitor present Charles Grundy, DI Gammon and myself DI Lee."

## The Poet And The Calling Card

"Miss Fiche, can I call you Rachel?" "If you wish Mr Gammon" "Ok Rachel, your affair with Annabelle Leaf, would you say it was a volatile relationship?" "You are making it out be some big love story and it wasn't, she was a bit besotted by me" "Ok so you were not that bothered?" "Correct. Look Annabelle was a nice girl, but she was well into the Church and her charity work, so I didn't see a lot of her".

"Would you say you had a temper Rachel, by that I mean do you flare up quite easily?" "No, but I will stick-up for myself like any normal person" "When did you realise your sexual tendencies were for women, not men, Rachel?" "I object Mr Gammon, my client's sexual preferences are nothing to do with anyone" "Oh but I think they are Mr Grundy".

"Are you jealous Rachel?" "No, why would I be? I told you Annabelle was more interested in me than I was her" "So the girl who you attacked in a nightclub in

# The Poet And The Calling Card

Hull and glassed in the face, that wasn't a temper brought on by jealousy?" Grundy looked at Fiche he clearly wasn't aware of this. "No comment" "So you don't want to comment on the fact you were found guilty and were incarcerated in Hull Prison". "No comment." "Rachel you are not doing yourself any favours here." "The next little incident involved a lady you lived with, called Sonia Blake, in Stoke-on-Trent. Is that correct?" "No comment." Again Grundy looked at Rachel in bewilderment. "This time you were locked away in Werrington, which is a Young Offenders prison, is that correct Rachel?" "No comment."

"You see Rachel, it appears to me and to the law of the land that you are a jealous, violent, individual that hit's out when things don't go your way. I will again reiterate you are not helping yourself with your answers. Did you kill Annabelle Leaf and bury her?" "No comment." The door

# The Poet And The Calling Card

opened to the interview room and Sergeant Milton called DI Gammon over. Milton whispered in Gammon's ear and passed him a plastic bag. Gammon thanked Milton and returned to the table. "Today we have done a full and concise search of your property, Number three Daisy Close and look what we have found, an orange envelope and one of my business cards. Would you like to explain to me, firstly about the Orange envelope? and secondly about my business card?"

"The Orange envelope was from a card I received on my birthday and I thought it was a lovely colour and was going to use the colour to emulsion my living room. B & Q mix paints to any colour you want" "Ok, and my business card?" "You left a business card on my table when you came to see me at work. If you look on the back it will say milk, eggs and bread. I wrote on the back what I had to pick up that night

# The Poet And The Calling Card

from the local shop." Gammon checked and yes it did say that.

"Ok, interview suspended pending further investigations. You are required to hand in your passport to Bixton Police and you are not allowed to move from your current address unless you contact the Police here at Bixton first" "You are bloody ridiculous, all this because some stupid little girl thinks she is a lesbian and gets herself killed" "Take her out of my site DI Lee. We will be in touch". 'What a hardnosed bitch' he thought. 'Let's hope the IT lads come up with something from Fiche's laptop.'

Gammon headed for the observation area to listen to Rinko Bolan's interview with DI Smarty and DI Fairfield.

"Mr Bolan now that we know your real name, we have asked you back for this interview because we have concerns about your ability to tell the truth. The sample of

# The Poet And The Calling Card

your hand writing, in an expert's opinion, says it isn't your natural hand. That you consistently try to hide how you write, we think there may be a link against the writings of the killer. The Orange envelopes are only sold locally and that is in a Polish shop you frequent. You were sacked from your job at Gosberton Pickers over an assault with another worker".

"He attacked me Mr Gammon, but he was local boy so they sack me" "Why did he attack you?" "I can't remember, something silly I think" "What, like almost killing his sister, that kind of silly?" Bolan broke down and cried. "So let's recap on what we have. You could have quite easily taken detective John Gammons business cards you had access. You have been violent to women in the past, on more than one occasion, and you came here illegally. Now why would I believe you are a changed man Mr Bolan?" "I was silly man in those days,

## The Poet And The Calling Card

drinking, taking drug, I am good man now with my Gina. Please, I don't do these terrible things" "Your house is being searched as we speak if anything turns up you will be brought back. You must leave your passport with Bixton Police and you are not allowed to move until we have been informed of your whereabouts, do I make myself clear?" Bolan was still crying and he mumbled. "Yes, thank you Sir, I am good man". Gammon watched his body language as he left and felt he believed Bolan, but he had been wrong before.

With both suspects now interviewed they were not really any further forward. It was now almost 9.30pm John was the last one left, other than Sergeant Yap, on the front desk. He was feeling quite hungry but also guilty that some young girl was probably in a shallow grave somewhere, tethered round her neck with piano wire, frightened

## The Poet And The Calling Card

to death and he didn't have a name for her or was any further forward with the cases.

John drove to the Tow'd Man hoping Saron would do him some food. The road to the Tow'd Man was quiet treacherous, there was a lot of black ice and they had given snow for the early hours of Sunday morning.

The Tow'd Man car park had already had a dusting of snow. To say the weather was quite bad, the pub was quite busy, a lot of the locals were in even the vicar from Pritwich. Matthew Spouncer was stood at the bar with half of Guinness. "Good evening Mr Gammon, how are you?" "Very well vicar, yourself?" "I can't complain Mr Gammon, we have just had the Christmas raffle for the surrounding villages. I tend to do here, at the Spinning Jenny, The Sycamore, and Up The Steps Maggie's quite a pleasurable part of my job Mr Gammon" "How long have you been at Pritwich vicar?" "Please call me

# The Poet And The Calling Card

Matt" "Well I'm John" and he put his hand out to shake it. John noticed the vicar had a tattoo on his right cuff. The vicar seemed ashamed of it and pulled his cuff down. "I have been here five years John. It's a lovely part of the country. I have been lucky enough to live in some beautiful parts of the country with my job".

"Would you like a drink Matt?" "Well I really should get off, Sunday's are always a busy day for me. I have three parishes in which to take services in". "Just a half of Guinness?" "Ok then, thank you John" "My pleasure".

Saron was a bit shocked to see John. "Thought you were going to Barcelona John?" "I did go but came back early for work" "Oh, I don't like the sound of that" "You know the score Saron. I'll have a pint of Micklock Mud and a half of Guinness for Matt please. Is there any chance you could do me a sandwich?"

## The Poet And The Calling Card

"Why not hang on until 11.00pm me and Angelina have a Chinese some Saturday nights" "Ok, put me down for a Singapore Chow Mein." "Extra hot I am guessing?" "You got it Saron".

John wandered back to Matthew Spouncer. "Not given good weather for tomorrow, John" "No how do you get about Matt?" "I have a Land Rover Defender, they get anywhere" "I bet they do" "So how did you end up in The Peak district John?" "It's a long story" "Time to own up" said the vicar "I have followed your career for a long time, I probably know more about you than you do" and he laughed. Spouncer's teeth were a bit crooked and John noticed a very large gold filling which he thought was quite unusual. He thought him to be about fifty, he had a good head of hair but was weathered as if he had worked outside a lot.

## The Poet And The Calling Card

"You are quite the hero in these parts John. I bet the criminals quake in their boots when they hear the name John Gammon" and Spouncer laughed. John wasn't sure of this guy, he seemed most unlike any vicar he had seen before, although he seemed to be well liked in the parishes. "Listen John, nice to have met you, it would be even nicer if I saw you in Church tomorrow as well though" and he smiled and left.

"Does he come in very often Saron?" "Odd time, not a lot. He gives me the creeps to be honest John. I can feel him staring at me and if I bend down to get a bottle or crisps or something he always has a comment. Angelina has said the same" "Mmmm came across to me as being a bit odd, but I just put it down to me not moving in his circles".

It was almost 10.30pm and the pub was just about empty, Saron came round the bar and sat with John. Saron always

## The Poet And The Calling Card

dressed immaculately, she had on a small white skirt, brown stilettos heels and brown blouse. She could have been going to a fashion show instead of working behind the bar at the Tow'd Man.

"So what happened in Barcelona?". He thought honesty was the best policy. "We arrived on the Friday and pretty much had a full day on the lash" "Well that isn't a surprise as you were with Piss Heads United hey?" "Poor Bob got in a real tangle, we played Jacks and he got most of the drinks, so Cheryl ended up taking him home, so everyone went back too. I wanted to stop out, so Jo's sister came along". John waited for Saron's reaction. She played it very cool. "So did you have a good night?" "Yes we did actually", then he thought he perhaps shouldn't over egg it. "Well it was ok" "So then what happened John?". John knew she meant, what happened next? but he drifted onto the next day. "Oh the Nou Camp John, bet

## The Poet And The Calling Card

you loved that, did Bob go?" "He made it but didn't look good, then I got a call from DCI Fringe telling me we had been contacted again by the killer. I decided I needed to get back" "You have always been committed John, even after the way you have been treated, I like that in a man".

Suddenly Angelina appeared with the Chinese. "Wow! That looks good" "We get it from The Oriental Palace in Bixton John and they deliver orders over twenty pounds, so you can't go wrong" "Bloody hell Mr Gammon, it's becoming a habit, you sat at this bar with my business partner". John retorted, "I can't think of anything nicer". Saron blushed.

Angelina finished her meal and said goodnight saving a cheeky wink at John as Saron's back was turned. "Are you staying John?". The invitation caught John off his guard. "Thanks for the offer Saron, but I have some bits I need to sort at home, you

## The Poet And The Calling Card

know post and that" "I understand, next time perhaps?" John kissed Saron tenderly on the lips and left for his cottage.

The weather was turning and a small flurry of snow started to fall as John opened his kitchen door. On the mat was his post and in the post an Orange envelope. John quickly opened it, inside was a message from the killer.

*"Hi John,*

*"How was Barcelona? Sorry it was ruined but you can't stop a man in his quest for notoriety. I told you there would be seven abductions and burials, then I promise to be a good boy. I can't say I will never torment you again, but I promise to stop after seven. It's a bit like the seven deadly sins I guess. Anyway you'll want a name? I hope your search for this lady isn't going*

## The Poet And The Calling Card

*too well, I don't want you having anymore successes than me!!!"*

*"Her name can be found on many a pump followed by heating your house you may find it here".*

*"Good luck John"*

*The Poet.*

John immediately called Donna Fringe. "Just received this in the post somewhere in it is the missing girls name Donna" "Ok look John, I haven't been out so I will go into the office and go through all the missing girls and see if it relates to anything. You get some sleep and I will see you in the morning, then you can take over if that's ok?" "Not a problem Donna" "I know it will be your day off, being a Sunday, so thanks" "Listen Donna I will work twenty four seven if it means the poor girl is found alive. I will see you in the morning". John cancelled the call

## The Poet And The Calling Card

poured himself a glass of Jameson's whisky and sat pondering the killer's information.

Pump he thought? Petrol pump? Bike pump? Central heating pump? John wrote down the names of all the leading brands so he could correlate his information with Donna the next day. Nothing made much sense and John retired to bed. Whoever is doing this, knows John's whereabouts and where he lives. Could Chi or his henchmen be tormenting him perhaps? He tossed and turned all night and woke at 7.00am feeling still tired. He quickly showered and headed for work. On the way he called at Beryl's Butties, but it was all boarded up with a sign saying closed for winter. 'That would never have happened in Beryl's day', he thought.

On the way to work he passed Maggie Else's home and he knew he had make time to talk to her about his half- sister

# The Poet And The Calling Card

who Horobin had found living in Colmar, France.

Gammon finally arrived at Bixton. "Good morning Di" "Good morning Sir, all quiet on the Western front". John liked Di Trimble she was always pleasant and was a good desk Sergeant.

"DCI Fringe said could you go to the incident room as soon as you arrive" "Thanks Di" Gammon headed for the incident room. "You look tired Donna" "I have trawled every missing girl in Derbyshire and nothing seems to tally up close, all I got was Christine Raleigh, I just thought 'bike pump'. When I chased it up the record hadn't been updated and she had been found living in Nottingham, so that was a waste of time. It does annoy me that these things are not updated" "Ok Donna, you get off and I will look further afield Yorkshire and Nottinghamshire" "Ok John, and thanks again for giving up your Sunday". "Not a problem, I will give

## The Poet And The Calling Card

you a call tonight and let you know how I get on" "Thanks John" and Donna left.

Gammon grabbed a coffee and set about trying to find a connection, it was almost 4.30pm when he came across a name, Stella Coles. She had been missing for three days. Her mother had called in to South Yorkshire Police, although she had stated Stella was a bit of a free spirit and would often go missing for a day or two. Gammon immediately called South Yorkshire Police.

"DI Arnold how can I help?". Gammon explained his reason for the call. "Think your luck may be in, Mrs Grant called in about an hour ago to say she had contacted all Stella's friends and they had not seen her since she left Toohy's bar on Murray Street in Rotherham around 10.00pm Thursday night." Gammon explained his thoughts and asked if it would be ok to

## The Poet And The Calling Card

interview Mrs Grant. "By all means we don't have the resources trying to find all these run aways, you country boys have much more time." Gammon didn't say anything as he wanted to keep on the right side of South Yorkshire Police. After he got Mrs Grant's address, he thanked DI Arnold.

Gammon left the station and called DCI Fringe on his way. "John, that's great news, do you think it's her?" "Yes I do Donna. I am on my way to talk to her mother" "Have you cleared it with the South Yorkshire Police John?" "Yes, it's all ok" "Brilliant, let me know in the morning and thanks again".

John put the address of Mrs Grant in his Sat Nav and set off. The weather was quite bad and the snow was coming down quite heavy. He arrived at Henley Drive, a large council estate on the outskirts of Rotherham. Gammon drove round for five minutes before coming across number

## The Poet And The Calling Card

thirty three. The house was not run down, like most of the others on the estate, but kept nicely. He knocked on the white PVC door. A woman in her late forties answered. "Can I help you?".

Gammon flashed his warrant card. "Mrs Grant? Can I come in?". "A voice from another room shouted, "Who is it Mavis?" "It's a detective from Derbyshire. Come through Mr Gammon. This is my hubby Glyn Grant." John thought he recognised him. "Well bloody hell, how are you John?" It suddenly hit him. "Whisky, how are you mate, still in the force?". Grant turned to his wife, "This John Gammon love, we did our initial training together all those years ago. You're bloody famous now aren't you John? and looking well I might say."

Gammon thought he could not say the same for Whisky, he was about four stone overweight, bald with at least two days stubble. "You still in the force then

## The Poet And The Calling Card

Whisky?" "No John, I am on disability pension now, got myself shot by some little tosser about ten year back in Rotherham city centre. It was one Sunday night they were raiding a chemist. That's how I met my missus Susie, she was a nurse and looked after me. She'd just been through a rough time, her husband had passed away about three months earlier and we kind of clicked and the rest is history. We've been married seven years now. So is this about Stella?" he asked. "Well I think so, I wouldn't normally tell you this but being an ex-colleague you would work it out anyway. We have a serial killer lose in Derbyshire and he is burying his victims alive and sending us clues. We have saved one girl out of three and the latest clue led me to you. I have to say I maybe miles out here and if that is the case let me apologies in advance. Stella may have just gone off, kids do it all the time. Can I ask you a few questions please?" "Of course do you mind if I call

# The Poet And The Calling Card

you Susie?" "Not a problem Mr Gammon" "John, please Susie"

"Ok so you reported Stella missing, when?" "Friday morning John" "Susie, had she ever done this before?" "To be honest, Stella is a bit of a free spirit since her father died. She idolised him. This is him on a charity do in Wales at the top of Snowdon. Simon was a Lay Preacher and a manager at the local Co-Op. He had a massive heart attack when he was in Tuscany, France with the church and Stella saw it all happen. I am afraid it affected her quite badly, she rebelled against the Church and from that day never went again. She is, what I think they call a Goth. She wears black satanic clothes and has tattoos and piercings everywhere. John, it's such a shame, this was the last picture of her taken with James, as they boarded the coach to go on that fateful church gathering in Tuscany"

# The Poet And The Calling Card

"How old was she there?" "She was eighteen John".

"So you have spoken with her friends Susie?" "Yes, we've phoned all her old school friends and her best mate who was with her that night and she said she'd left her about 10.30pm. They had been in Toohy's nightclub in Rotherham" "Have you got an address for her friend and a name?" "Yes her name is Mickey Bloom, well that's what Stella called her, but I think her real name is Mary but she liked to be called Mickey".

"What is her address?" "It's The Vicarage, Smidgley-over-Twain, it's about five miles from here. She lives with her parents. He is a vicar, that's how these two met when they were little. His name is Reverend Don Bloom and his wife Is Lisa Bloom, very big into their charities. I don't see much of them since my husband died, they were more his friends than mine John".

# The Poet And The Calling Card

"Ok, thanks for your help, I could be barking up the wrong tree so don't be worrying yourself Susie, she will probably contact you soon anyway. If she does, please let me know. In between times, I will speak with her mate. Great to see you Whisky" said John. "He won't tell me, why do you call him Whisky?" "After the whisky, made by Grants. With his surname being Grant, we christened him Whisky. Ok you two, I will be in touch" and John left.

As he drove away he was thinking 'but for the grace of God go I'. Whisky was top of his class and an excellent officer really destined for great things in the force and he had been reduced to what he was now. 'Feeling lucky' he thought.

Gammon decided to leave the chat with Mickey until the morning. He wanted to speak with Maggie Else and tell her about her daughter. John finally arrived back at Hittington at 10.20pm. He rang the

## The Poet And The Calling Card

doorbell hoping Maggie would still be up. The housemaid answered the door. "Mr Gammon, so nice to see you". "Is Miss Else still up?" asked John. "Yes come through". Maggie still looked good for her age a cross between Joanna Lumley and Honor Blackman he thought.

"Hello John, how lovely to see you. Would you like a drink? I am having a nice sherry". "Yes I will Maggie, it's been a long day" "Have you been at work?" "Yes, I've just finished". "Oh you poor thing, you'd better have a large sherry then" and she poured John a large sherry from the cut glass decanter. "There, sit down, I am so pleased you have called again". "Listen Maggie, I know you don't want to have anything to do with the daughter you gave up for adoption, but she is all I have left of a family so I have made some investigations and I have found her". Maggie looked frightened, but also slightly pleased, John thought. "Where is

## The Poet And The Calling Card

she John?" "She lives in Colmar, in France which is quite close to the German border". "What's her name?" "Fleur Fournier. That was her married name Maggie. She had been married and when she divorced, she went back to her maiden name Dubois". "Does she have children?" "No Maggie she doesn't. Do you want to see a picture of her?" Maggie hesitated but then her inquisitiveness got the better of her and she said yes. John pulled out a picture of Fleur that Saul Horobin had taken. Immediately tears streamed down her face. "She is so like you and Graham it's unbelievable. So you haven't met yet?" "No, I have so much on at work, I thought I may go and try and see her over Christmas". "John, just be aware she may reject you" "I know Maggie, but I have to try". They sat talking, Maggie was pleased he had called. It was just gone twelve when John left Maggie's house promising to get back in touch soon.

# The Poet And The Calling Card

The drive to his cottage was quite bad, there was about four inches of snow and it was drifting in places. John lay in bed that night thinking that maybe Stella was buried somewhere, who knew where, and the clock was ticking.

The first thing he did the next day was to get Donna Fringe back up to speed. He explained he hadn't called her as it had been too late last night. "Good work John, now we have to crack the poem? What the hell can he mean by "DROP"?". Gammon suddenly looked at Donna and it hit him like a hammer. "Bloody hell Donna what is our victim called?" "We think, Stella Coles you said" "There is a pub called 'The Last Drop' it's in Ardwalk, it closed in about nineteen seventy three. An old lady had it for many years, it was part of her farm, when she died it was just left to go ruin" "Still not getting it John". "What do they sell in pubs?" "Beer?" "Only

## The Poet And The Calling Card

bloody Stella Artois" "And your point is John?" "The pub and farm sit on what we, as kids called, Coles Hill, and what is Stella's surname? Coles. Come on we are wasting time let's go and see what we can find".

With haste DCI Fringe and Di Gammon headed for Ardwalk. Ardwalk was situated a few miles from Hittington and was a beautiful little hamlet of farms. Gammon's friends Shelley and Jack lived there. Jack had farmed there all his life and knew the area like the back of his hand. "Donna I need to speak with someone first".

They pulled up at Jack and Shelley's place. "Hey John, come in, would you like a piece of ginger cake? It's fresh out of the oven not ten minutes ago" "No thanks Shelley, is Jack about?" Shelly Called through to the back, "Jack, John is here. So why did you leave us in Barcelona? It got worse for Bob, Steve got him drunk again after you left and he ended up falling

# The Poet And The Calling Card

over and had concussion". Jack Appeared, "Hey up lad are you alright?" "Jack, Shelley, this is my boss DCI Fringe". "Pleased to meet you both" she said. "The Last Drop Inn, are we safe to go in?" "If you are careful, I will take you in if you want. There's not much left of the roof and the floors will be slippery with all this snow we have had" "Not a problem Jack, lead the way" "See you soon John, nice to have met you DCI Fringe" "Likewise" and they left Shelley at the door. Jack took them from his farmhouse up some very old stone steps. "Mind yourself they are probably a bit icy. Nobody comes up here anymore". They walked across two fields and in the snow John could see prints from the side of the house.

"What's that Jack?" "Dunno, I would be surprised if anybody has been up here, especially in this weather". There were also footprints of about a size ten or eleven, leading away from the old pub. By

## The Poet And The Calling Card

that John deduced somebody had been in the building prior to it snowing. Gammon had the feeling that this was the place.

"Jack you can leave us no, if you don't mind mate, this could be a crime scene". Donna radioed for Forensics and a couple more officers to come and help with the search. "The Poet is playing with us Donna, they have all been buried and I don't think this one is".

They entered the old building. In one corner the old dart board still hung, the bar was covered in pigeon muck and it smelt musty. There were even a couple of pictures. Although almost obliterated, Gammon could see a picture of his dad, Phil, in a darts team picture. Donna shouted John. "Help me lift this John". The cellar door had recently been disturbed. It was a heavy trap door, but John managed to lift it. "Did you bring a torch Donna?" "Of course, we women are

## The Poet And The Calling Card

always prepared, as they say in the Girl Guides".

John shone the torch down into the cellar, he could see old barrels and empty bottles covered in dust and cobweb's. The steps down were a bit precarious and John gingerly went down into the cellar, unaware of what lay before him. Donna was next down. The cellar area had two small rooms off the main area.

They looked round the main room nothing other than a mess. Gammon opened the door to the first small room, again nothing. Donna turned the door knob on the second room suddenly the door flung open as if on a strong spring. Donna screamed as she entered the room Gammon came running over. Donna was lay in heap, there was the headless corpse of a woman, lay on the floor and a head swinging on piano wire, dripping blood above them. Somehow the killer had rigged the room so whoever opened the door set of a sequence of

## The Poet And The Calling Card

events that decapitated the victim. Gammon could do nothing for the victim and tried to bring Donna round. He was glad he had sent Jack on his way. John phoned the station and explained the situation to DI Smarty and Forensics. Donna started to come round just as Di Smarty and DI Cus'tard arrived with Forensics.

"All yours Wally, worse one yet" "I get all the best jobs John". "Whoever the killer is, I believe was here yesterday and I think the tracks outside are our killers, so I want that area looking at in some detail Wally and answers for tomorrow please" "You are a hard task master Mr Gammon". "Just get on with it Wally, I need conformation that this is Stella Coles, if possible mate" "Leave it with me, we will do our best". "Smarty, Cus'tard, door knocking time, ask around the houses close to here to see if anyone has seen anything suspicious, such has a car or van parked close by, or

## The Poet And The Calling Card

somebody suspicious hanging around. Ok I will see you later at the station".

"I'll drive us back Donna" "I killed that poor girl John, the killer knew that could happen, it was set up" "You weren't to know that Donna" "That poor girl, I can't get her features out of my head, how can somebody do this John? What is wrong with people?" "If we knew that, there would be no need for people like us Donna".

"Did you say, if it's Stella, she is the stepdaughter of an old colleague?" "Yes, Whisky Grant, and to be honest it looks like he has had ten years of hell. Now his lovely wife has this to contend with if it's Stella".

It was almost 3.30pm when they arrived back at Bixton. Donna was still shook up. "Look why don't we call it a day, we can't do anything until the forensic lads have sorted their side out" "Good idea John, are

## The Poet And The Calling Card

you going for a drink?" "Well I certainly can do" "I need a brandy to calm me down". "Come on then, I'll take you to the Spinning Jenny" "That's where we are having our Christmas party isn't it?" "Yes, great boozer, you will like Kev and Doreen".

They arrived at the Spinning Jenny, Kev was full of talk about Barcelona and what had happened to Bob. John introduced Donna. "Oh, so this is the wicked witch that made you leave early?" and he laughed. "He is only joking Donna" "Only my bit of fun Donna" said Kev and Donna smiled. "What can I get you both?" "Two double brandies please Kev and one for you mate" "Very kind of you John, I'll just have a half, if that's ok?".

Donna dropped the double brandy and two more after that. "Can we sit down John?". They sat in the corner. "Do you want some food John?". Suddenly Donna burst into tears. "Hey, Hey, come on, none of this is

## The Poet And The Calling Card

your fault Donna" "It is John, I opened that door and severed that poor girls head" "How were you to know he had duct-taped her mouth shut so she couldn't try and warn you? It could have been me opening that door, I just happened to open the first door. It's just one of those things". Kev came over at this point. "Are you alright love?" "Donna had a major shock at work today" answered John, "Here let me get you some more brandy, it will help". Kev wasn't great in these situations, so he brought two more double brandies over, then left them and scurried back behind the bar.

"John that was the worst thing I have ever seen in all my years in the force". "Look Donna, you have to move on. For some reason, this sick bastard set this up. I don't know why, but what I do know is, he will slip up at some point of that I have no doubt and when he does we will be waiting".

## The Poet And The Calling Card

"Good evening Sir, good evening Ma'am" "Oh Hi Carl, Joni how are you both?" "Good thanks". "Carl, please call me Donna out of work" "And you know to call me John out of work". "Sorry about that it's just habit". "So who is this pretty young lady Carl?" asked Donna. "This is Joni". Carl was just about to say, my girlfriend, when Joni interrupted him and said 'A good friend'. She gave John the smile and he knew what she was on with. "Would you like to join us?"

"No, but thanks for the offer Donna, we are having a meal then getting back, but have a nice evening and thanks again for the offer", with that Joni and Carl moved to the bar. "Seems like a nice girl John?". John thought it best not to mention they had once had a relationship, so he did the sensible thing and just said 'yes'.

"So is this your local John?" "Well I use possibly four different ones depending, on how I am feeling". "What about you

## The Poet And The Calling Card

Donna?" "Well since I got here, it's just been work, work, work. Not really had chance to sort a social life out. My parents live in Conksderry, so when I had the chance to move I did" "Not married then Donna?" "No I was in a long term relationship, but we split up eighteen month ago. It was never going to be, he couldn't handle me being in the job" "What did he do for a living?" "Brian was a Civil Engineer. What about you?" "I was married to Lindsay, we lived in London, it's a long story but we divorced some time ago". Both of us free and single then?". Normally John would have took the bait, but the last time he had an affair with his boss, it ended in tears so he thought he would play this one cool.

The brandy was having an effect on Donna. "Where are you living Donna?" "I have just rented the Old Post Office Cottage in Hittington" "Now that is a coincidence, that's where I lived before I

## The Poet And The Calling Card

moved to Mum's farm" "How long ago John?" "Just a while ago". "Oh, not sure it's the same place, they said a woman rented it but she now ran a pub". 'Bugger' John thought now, he had to explain about Saron. "That's correct I lived with Saron, who now runs the Tow'd Man pub" "That's an unusual name, I saw that on a document at the station" "Yes Saron was in Forensics, that's how we met"

He could see the disdain in Donna's body language. "We split but are still good friends." He was just hoping that somehow Sandra Scooper's name didn't come into the equation.

Lo and behold the next words out of Donna's mouth, was that Sandra had come to see her to explain she was pregnant and was having it quite rough with morning sickness. "I have taken her off front line duties John, it's too much of a risk. I didn't like to be nosey, but she doesn't wear a wedding ring, is she not married?"

## The Poet And The Calling Card

"No Donna" "Oh she lives with somebody then does she?" John was really on the spot now. Time to act dumb he thought. "Couldn't tell you Donna". "Anyway, that's the score with Sandra. Look the brandy is having a bit of an effect on me, could you get me a taxi home".

John made his way to the bar. "Kev can you book a taxi for Donna to Hittington please". "No problem mate".

Joni was sat on her own at the bar. "You not going with her John?" "No why would I?" "Well only you would know that, but it's a bit out of character don't you think?" John was about to give it Joni back when Carl appeared. "Are you ready Joni? it's flippin' freezing out there. Good night John" "Yes goodnight Carl". "See you around John" and Joni smiled at him.

Donna's taxi arrived. Old Phil had been running taxis from the village since John was a lad. "Goodnight Donna, try and get

## The Poet And The Calling Card

some sleep". "Thanks for the company John, appreciate that" "Anytime, you know that."

John went up to the bar it was almost 11.30pm, so he had one last pint with Kev, whilst Kev told him what happened to Bob in Barcelona.

"Right mate, I'm off for some kip see you soon" "Good to see you John". John arrived at his cottage just before midnight. Waiting on the mat was an orange envelope. John opened it.

*"Dear John,*

*See you found the girl. Sorry it was a bit messy but you have to learn I won't be beat. If it's any consolation to you she was dying anyway so I just slipped her some coke and she was away with the fairies while I set up the wires.*

# The Poet And The Calling Card

*I might not do anymore until the New Year I will let you have your Christmas. I mean everyone deserves a Christmas don't they?*

*I have to say you were quite clever to work this one out so quickly but you are a clever sod anyway. I will be in touch".*

**The Poet**

John didn't sleep well that night knowing he had the dreadful job of telling somebody they had lost a loved one the next day.

The Freelander made good headways in the snow but the main roads into Bixton were strewn with lorries and cars that had skidded off the road.

Gammon arrived at Bixton and headed straight to DCI Fringes office. He showed her the letter "I will give it Forensics, but it's doubtful they will find anything. You

## The Poet And The Calling Card

ok Donna?" "I feel bloody dreadful, would you mind if I went back home? I can't function like this" "Not a problem". Gammon was quite pleased he enjoyed running things. "Thanks John, I owe you one".

Gammon called the meeting with everyone and Forensics. "Ok Wally, what you got for me?" "Well first thing, in her jeans pocket she had your calling card John, but we have come to expect that. Her dental records show her to be Stella Coles, she was reported missing by South Yorkshire Police. She was a drugs user, but on the evidence I have found so far, not a long time user, although there were traces of cocaine in her system. She had been tethered by very sharp razor wire and that was how she died. She was alive prior to the contraptions being triggered. She had not eaten for at least three days. From what we can see, no sexual contact is evident. My gut feeling is she knew her

# The Poet And The Calling Card

killer John. There are no bruises and she doesn't appear to have struggled" "Ok thanks.

Ok, what have we got other than four John Gammon business cards? We have the same pattern every time. I get an orange envelope with a poem or riddle, I then get another one later with a riddle to sort her name, this is generally sent to my house".

"Right I want twenty four seven surveillance from the barn across from my house, if we see anyone delivering a letter, I want them apprehending". "Even the postman?" "I said anyone didn't I? Our killer may dress as a postman to deliver the orange envelope, so watch what he puts in the letterbox, if it's orange we arrest. Are we clear?". They all agreed. "Ok, so the list of victims so far are is:-

Mandy Nichol - Dead

Michelle Wilkinson - Alive

The Poet And The Calling Card

Annabelle Leaf - Dead

Stella Coles - Dead

"As you can see, our success rate is of concern. Di Smarty, Cus'tard and Fairfield, get working on these four girls, let's see if we can find any connections. We do have Michelle Wilkinson alive, she may be able to help but please use kid gloves, she has had a traumatic time. We appear to have hit a dead end on the envelopes. Sergeant Milton, I would like you to dig some more on Rinko Bolan. I want you to go to Poland, speak with the local police and his neighbours, let's build a profile of this man".

"DI Cooper, I want you to go to Hull and interview Sonia Blake one of Rachel Fiche's victims. DI Lee, let's see if the footprints in the snow could have been our killer, work with Wally on this".

## The Poet And The Calling Card

"Ok, thanks everybody, let's get to it". Gammon told Sergeant Yap he was going up to Rotherham to inform Stella Coles mother of the findings and also to inform South Yorkshire Police they could close the missing person case. He would explain that he would break the sad news to Stella's mother. "Will do. Good luck Sir". Said Yap

It had started snowing again as John headed over to Rotherham to deliver the bad news. He arrived at 3.20pm the sky was full of snow and he knew he better not stay long or he might not get back.

John rang the doorbell of the neat council house. Susie came to the door. "Hey John come in, Whisky will be so chuffed you have called. I was so pleased, I was going to call you, but it's good of you to come all this way". John looked a bit bemused. "Why was that Susie?" "Your colleague DI Poet rang about thirty minutes ago to say you had found Susie and she had said

## The Poet And The Calling Card

she will be home for Christmas, I can't thank you enough John" "Yes thanks John, you are a good mate coming all this way in this weather" said Whisky. "Just a minute Susie, sit down. I am afraid we found your daughter yesterday, but she is dead, the man that rang you is the killer". "No John, he told me". "This man is very sick Susie, he is playing with your mind. I would not tell you this if I wasn't one hundred percent certain".

Susie fell into Whisky's arms sobbing. "I failed her when her dad died, I was in such a mess and I should have been there for her" "Susie I'm sure you didn't. Would you like me to get a bereavement councillor over to sit with you?" "We will be fine John, thank you". "Look mate I am so sorry for your loss, but I am afraid Susie still has to formally identify the body. Do you need me to send a car over for you in the morning?" "No John we have transport." "Good to see you mate,

## The Poet And The Calling Card

sorry it's been in such tragic circumstances. I may need to speak further with Susie" "Understand John, you get off, the weather is bad". With that John left them to grieve.

The Poet was now playing John. How did he know he would be going over to see Whisky and Susie? How was he getting this information?

Gammon informed Donna with regard to what had happened. She was still feeling rough, she said. "Never drinking with you again John" "Did you sleep ok?" "Like a baby" "Well it was worth it then. Ok Donna I will see you in the morning".

The weather by now was getting quite bad, so John headed straight home. The roads leading down to the farm were treacherous by now, there was quite a build-up of snow. The Council Gritting team were out in force but they appeared to be losing the battle.

## The Poet And The Calling Card

John grabbed his shovel and cleared a path to his front door. Cold and wet he finally got into his warm snug living room. John decided to make notes to see if he could see anything that might have associated the girls.

He poured a large Jameson's and sat in his favourite chair scribbling on his pad. Outside the snow was falling big flakes the size of marshmallows. Suddenly John clicked. The first victim, Mandy Nichol, from a poor background, maybe this one was a mistake? The second girl, Michelle Wilkinson, had charity and church involvement. The third victim, Annabelle Leaf, also charity work and church connections. The fourth victim, Stella Cole, her father was a lay preacher and she used to attend Church. That's the bloody connection, I'm sure of it, just Mandy Nichol seems to be the odd one out. John wrote Church connection on his pad. Now

## The Poet And The Calling Card

why my business cards and why only contact me?

John sat for two hour's trying to think where a connection could be. He wasn't a churchgoer but he did believe. His Mum had been a big Churchgoer, was that the connection? he thought. With all this in mind John decided to call Matthew Spouncer, the local vicar who found the first body. "Reverend Spouncer? John Gammon here, sorry it's a bit late to call you, I just wondered if you would mind helping us with our inquiries on the murder cases we have? I feel I may have a connection" Spouncer sounded nervous. "Well I'm not sure how I can help Mr Gammon" "Pop down to the station or I can call round to the vicarage if you prefer?" "Ok say about 11.00am in the morning. You know where the vicarage is Mr Gammon?" "Yes, it's up Slippery Lane in Pritwich or it was?" "Yes that's right Mr Gammon, I will see you at

## The Poet And The Calling Card

11.00am". John felt that he may be onto something. It was almost 11.40pm and half a bottle of Jameson had been consumed when John climbed the stairs. He quickly checked the weather and could see all his tracks were completely covered.

The following morning around 7.40am there was a knock on John's door. John was up making a coffee. "Hello Roger how are you?" "Good thanks John, just to let you know we have been up with the tractor and cut away out onto the road. The roads don't look too bad John" "Roger you are a star thanks very much. Do you and your lad want me to bring a coffee and a bacon sandwich over to the milking parlour?" "That would be good John, thank you". "Least I can do Roger".

John set to making Roger and his son a couple of bacon sandwiches and a big mug of coffee each. He walked across the yard and into the milking parlour. He placed the sandwiches and coffee on the side and

## The Poet And The Calling Card

shouted to Roger and his lad. "Thanks John we will just finish milking and have it" "No problem mate and thanks again for digging out". As John walked out of the milking shed it evoked happy memories of his time with Adam, helping Phil at weekends and after school during the week. 'Such great innocent times' he thought as he wandered back.

John grabbed his phone, keys and lap top and headed to Pritwich to see Reverend Spouncer. On the way he phoned DCI Fringe to fill her in with his thoughts.

Pritwich vicarage was quite old built around 1820 there was quite a long drive up to the house and the building was covered in creeping ivy to the west side. John could remember, as a child, going to garden parties held there in the summer with Steve Lineman. Quite often the pair of them would take buns and pop from the Women's Institute tent. John would wait outside around the back of the tent and

# The Poet And The Calling Card

Steve would pretend he was in the SAS scrambling along on his belly. It's a wonder they were never caught.

John knocked on the old oak door which felt like bell metal. After a few seconds Reverend Spouncer came to the door. "Do come in Mr Gammon". Matthew Spouncer was in his mid-forties with dark hair greying at the side's. John's Mum used to say he looked distinguished. Spouncer showed John into the drawing room. The house was massive and John thought how lonely it must be rattling around this place. "Tea Mr Gammon?" "That would be great Reverend". "Please call me Matt" "Ok, thanks Matt" "I will be back shortly, please take a seat". In the corner was a baby grand piano, all-round the edge of the oak panelled room, were books on various religions. Adorning part of one wall were photographs that looked like they were taken on charity travels to various places. John could hear him

## The Poet And The Calling Card

coming back, so he sat down in the green leather winged chair.

"There you go Mr Gammon". The reverend had made a pot of tea with scones. "How can I help you Mr Gammon? Is it regarding that poor girl I stumbled across in the Churchyard? Only I have given a statement to your colleagues already" "I would just like your input, we appear to have a common thread going on with these murders, other than the first one, all the girls were either churchgoers or had been and I was wondering if you may have known any of them?"

Gammon laid out four pictures of the girls. Matthew Spouncer looked at each one but was very dismissive. "Can't say I do Mr Gammon" "Are you sure? Would you like to take another look?". This question seemed to unnerve Spouncer. He looked again. "That girl maybe, I have her seen at a summer camp or something, not sure". Spouncer had picked out Annabelle Leaf,

# The Poet And The Calling Card

she was possibly about sixteen in the picture. Gammon thought it strange that Spouncer had suddenly remembered this girl. After probably twenty minutes of awkward questions Spouncer announced he had to be at Dilley Dale Church for a coffee morning. Gammon thanked him for his time. "If I need to talk again, would you prefer here or at the station Matt?" "Oh here is fine Mr Gammon". The phone rang. "Please excuse me a minute". Gammon took his chance to get another look at the pictures on the wall. He quickly took some pictures of a few of them and one in particular of Spouncer and another guy on top of Snowdon in Wales, he thought he recognised the other guy.

Spouncer came back in. "Sorry to rush you Mr Gammon, but you know how tetchy these women's institutes can get if you are late" "Not a problem Matt, thanks for your time" "Go steady on the roads Mr

# The Poet And The Calling Card

Gammon, they look quite bad" "You too Matt".

Gammon got in his Freelander and set off for the station.

As he was driving along he was trying to think where he had seen the other guy in the picture. "Morning John". Sandra had just pulled up. "Just been for another scan to see how far gone I am". John felt embarrassed he felt like he was letting Sandra down and to some degree he was. "Everything ok?" "So far, so good, John. I have told DCI Fringe" "Yes she told me, you are doing desk duties aren't you?" "So she said. I will miss the front line but the baby is more important". There was an awkward silence but luckily Sergeant Milton was walking across to one of the cars. "Morning Sir" "Morning Carl you ok?" "Well other than DCI Fringe kicking off, apparently Chan Chi has been spotted in Derby". "Excuse me Sandra, best get in and find out what's going on". Gammon

## The Poet And The Calling Card

left Milton and Scooper looking bemused as he made a quick exit.

Gammon met a very aggravated DCI Fringe. "Chi has been spotted in Derby John" "Where Donna?" "Apparently he was in an Indian restaurant in Finch Street. An ex-police officer recognised him but didn't do anything, he waited to see what was happening, as something was kicking off with the owner of the restaurant. The ex-copper Malcolm Clem over heard a conversation about the owner and protection money, apparently the restaurant had been a bit quiet with the lead up to the Christmas period. He told Chi that he could not afford to pay everything that week. Chi apparently said you have been told and left. Ex-Sergeant Clem wanted to follow him, but he argued with his wife who said it had nothing to do with him, by the time he got outside Chi had gone "So now what?" "Well it gets worse, in the early hours of this morning

## The Poet And The Calling Card

the restaurant was set alight. One of the chefs slept there overnight and was burned alive. It's going to be all over Sky news in about an hour and my boss wants to know where we are on finding this Psycho. Chi is giving us the run-around I need to get officers into Derby to find this man and if that means the murder case suffers then so be it"

"But Donna, I am finding things out" said John. "Ok well you stop on the murder case. Everyone else is on the Chi case". With that Donna flounced off, clearly rattled.

'Great' John thought 'now what?'. He went to his office, he had very little post to open, so sat pondering the vicar's photographs and who was the mystery man with Spouncer on top of Snowdon. He decided to take a break so he grabbed a sandwich and a coffee and sat looking at best ways to get to Colmar between Christmas and the New Year. Hopefully,

## The Poet And The Calling Card

to try and see his half-sister. There was a chance she maybe there or not, but the suspense was killing him. There was a flight into Strasbourg International Airport on December 27th returning December 29th so John booked it and also booked the hire car. He sat feeling quite pleased with himself, this was it, now he had to go.

John finished his sandwich, as he bent down to put the wrapping into the bin he suddenly realised where he had seen the picture. It was the one Susie had shown him when he went to see her and Whisky the first time.

Gammon grabbed his coat and told Scooper he wouldn't be back today. Gammon headed back to Rotherham to see if the picture on the phone was as he thought, the same as the one on the sideboard at Susi and Whisky's house.

John arrived at the house and rang the bell. Whisky came to the door. "Hello John,

## The Poet And The Calling Card

come in". The house wasn't as tidy as previously. "Susie is in Carmarthen, Wales at her sisters for a few days, she isn't handling this business at all well. I see you have got John Walvin working with you up there. Thank him next time you see him, he was very good with Susie. We didn't realise that Stella's head had been severed" "Sorry she was in a mess Whisky, but guess that was always going to be, no parent wants to bury their children". "No it's a sad time mate, I mean, don't get me wrong she had given me and her Mum the run around. I think she thought I was trying to take Simon's place and I know that could never be and she rebelled quite a bit"

"How did she die John? You were a bit vague, so I am guessing it was grisly". Gammon explained what had happened. "Hey no blame on anyone other than the bastard that did it mate. Well I am sure this isn't just a social visit is it?" "I need to

## The Poet And The Calling Card

check something Whisky, if that's ok?". Gammon pulled out his phone and loaded the picture he had taken at Matthew Spouncer's house and bingo they matched.

"Do you know Reverend Spouncer John? Nice chap, he used to come round and talk with Stella in the early days to try and get her back on track. He had been big mates with Simon apparently" "Really Whisky? that's interesting" "You don't think he had something to do with this do you?" "I really don't know, but he told me he didn't know Stella when I showed him her picture" "Now that is odd John. Funnily enough I think Susie was going to contact him about doing the service for Stella" "Well mate, don't say anything, that will make it interesting" "Of course I won't John".

Whisky made John a coffee and they spent a good hour reminiscing about the past. "Do you remember Claire Assist? She had the hot's for you and what a stunner she

## The Poet And The Calling Card

was John" "Yeah I did take her out a couple of times, think she made a DCI. The last time heard she lives down Norfolk or somewhere like that" "We wouldn't get away with the suggestive remarks we made to her these days" "You are right there Whisky, you can't say anything these days. Look mate good to see you as always, I best make my way back" "Yes John, good to see you mate. I will make a few inquiries on Reverend Spouncer, discreetly of course John" "Well here mate, that's my card, let me know if you find anything" "Will do John". John waved goodbye and set off back to the Peak District.

He decided on the Tow'd Man for an evening meal. John arrived just after 6.00pm Angelina was serving a couple of holiday makers. "Evening Mr Gammon" "Good evening Angelina, to what do we owe this pleasure?" "If you have come to see Saron, she is staying at her Mum's

## The Poet And The Calling Card

tonight. She has had a bit of a fall, nothing serious, but she thought she best stop overnight, so we have got Mike cooking tonight. You just will have to do with me for sparkling conversation John". Angelina looked well, she had dark black figure hugging trousers, with a loose fitting white blouse, they complimented her figure well and of course the cheeky smile she always gave John.

"So what are you having?" "I'll have a pint of Twitchers Throstle and Lasagne with garlic bread and salad". "Ok, but just one thing John" "What's that?" "You do realise you can't kiss a lady with Garlic breath" and she laughed passing John his pint and strolling off to the kitchen with John's order.

John parked himself at the bar. Angelina returned. "Are you going to sit there and keep me company Mr Gammon?" John decided attack was the best policy. "Well yes, but the real reason is to admire that

## The Poet And The Calling Card

figure" and he smiled. "Touché" she said "I will behave now I promise". The pub was very quiet, a young couple and a pair of walkers and they had all gone by 9.00pm. John was just thinking about leaving when Angelina came round from behind the bar with two large brandies. "To good friends" and she raised her glass, John did the same "Good Friends"

The drinking had started, it was 12.55am, when Angelina asked John if he could take her upstairs, undress her and put her to bed. John was thinking, 'should he or not?'. But John being John took his chance.

John switched off the pub lights. Angelina said she needed the toilet. John checked the doors then climbed the stairs to Angelina's room, the only one at the top of the stairs with a light on. He walked in, no sign of Angelina then he turned round. She had stripped down to her underwear, which left nothing to John's imagination.

# The Poet And The Calling Card

Soon they were in a hot embrace, she stripped John and they were rolling about on the King Size bed. They thought it was wrong, but neither was going to give this chance up. After fulfilling their lust, Angelina lay on John's chest.

"Well?" "Well what?" "Do you have any regrets John?" "About what we have just done?", he said. "Well of course Silly" "No I am a free agent and so are you, I assume?" "I guess. Can I ask you something John, well two things actually?" "If you want" "Are you still keen on Saron?" "Look, I will be honest, if I hadn't have been married and hurt, then I probably would have been engaged to Saron now but I can't commit" "Ok, well the second one is up to you if you answer" "Go on then" "Sandra Scooper is pregnant isn't she?" "I believe so" "And it's yours I guess?" "One question too far Angelina" "Thought so" and she smiled.

## The Poet And The Calling Card

They fell asleep and John woke at 7.15am his usual time. Angelina was downstairs cooking breakfast. John wandered down. "Look I would prefer you didn't mention this to Saron" "I'm not that brave John, she is still madly in love with you, so get your breakfast and don't worry about it". Was Angelina telling me she wanted a casual affair? John thought.

John finished his breakfast and thanked Angelina for a nice night, pecked her on the cheek and left. He had only gone down the lane probably six hundred yards, when a green mini-clubman, which he knew to be Saron's, was coming the other way. Saron flashed her headlights and put her hand up. 'Bloody hell that was close' he thought.

John carried on down to the cottage to get changed for work. Phyllis Swan, John's cleaner, had just pulled up. "Morning Mr Gammon" "Morning Phyllis, how are you?" "Oh not so bad, well could be

## The Poet And The Calling Card

better, so much work on the farm and now Billy has a bad knee and is struggling to get about" "Look if this cleaning job is too much I understand" "Not likely Mr Gammon, gets me out of the farm for a couple of hours" "Well I appreciate what you do for me Phyllis" "I enjoy doing it Mr Gammon". "Right, I'll just get a quick shower and get changed for work Phyllis" "No problem John, plenty to be getting on with down here".

John showered and changed and set off for work. Di Trimble was on the front desk. "I thought Sandra was doing the desk for now Di?" "She phoned in sick Sir" "Oh ok"

Donna called John into her office. "What did you find out John?" "Right well the murdered girl, Stella Coles, was the step-daughter of an old mate, we started in the force together. Yesterday I spent a morning with the local vicar, one Matthew Spouncer. Gammon pinned his picture to

## The Poet And The Calling Card

the board. I have a theory that three out of the four victims are connected by the Church. I questioned Spouncer, showed him pictures of the victims and he said he didn't recognise anyone. While he was out of the room, I took some pictures of pictures on the walls and one in particular of him with a guy stood on top of Snowdon. When I went to see Whisky, my ex colleague and step father to Stella Coles, his wife was out so we sat chatting. I showed him the pictures and he knew straight away who he was and who the other guy was with Spouncer"

"So who is he?" "He is the father of Stella Coles and clearly a big former friend of the Reverend Spouncer" "Are you bringing him in for questioning John?" "Well apparently Mrs Coles wants our Reverend Spouncer to take the service at Stella's funeral. I suggest we put twenty four hour surveillance on him Donna" "Can't John, I don't have the resources or

## The Poet And The Calling Card

the budget" "So we let him kill again if indeed it is him?" "That's it John, you have no evidence as such" "The man gives me the creeps, there is more to him than meets the eye" "All I can say is keep digging John. Thank you". John shut the office door on the way out.

Gammon went down to Forensics to see Wally. "Any luck on the footprints?" "Could be anybody John, the boots are walking boots made by Rocky Foot, a very well-known brand, and they are size ten, a very common size. So in answer to your question, it is a waste of time. Nothing found in the shed or on the wire. Absolutely nothing John". "What about Rachel Fiche's laptop?" "Nothing John, clean as a whistle, whoever is doing this, are meticulous in their planning". It wasn't what Gammon wanted to hear but he knew Wally would have checked everything, so if he said there was nothing, there was nothing. "Ok thanks Wally".

# The Poet And The Calling Card

Feeling a bit disappointed, Gammon went back to his office, on the way Di Trimble asked for some money for the Christmas Bash at the Spinning Jenny. "Blimey is it that close to Christmas Di?" "It is, two and a half weeks to go. This year we have got Tony Baloney doing the disco, its fifteen pound a head, including the buffet. How many would you like Sir?" "Just the one this year" said John. "Oh?" Di Trimble seemed a bit caught off guard. "I will be there this year, with DI Scooper doing the desk, it will be my first time in ages as I'm usually working Sir". Gammon handed over his money. "There you go Sir, December 16$^{th}$ from 7.30pm at The Spinning Jenny" "Look forward to it Di".

Gammon carried on up the stairs to his office. Nothing much was in the post, so he filled out his reports, which some were over a month old. Filling forms in was never Gammon's strong point. Just after lunch Gammon decided to go and see the

# The Poet And The Calling Card

only surviving victim, Michelle Wilkinson, to see if she had remembered anything new to the investigation.

John pulled up at The Limes in Foxhouses. He knocked on the door and Bob Wilkinson, the father, came to the door. "Inspector Gammon, how lovely to see you, do come in. Michelle, Inspector Gammon is here". Michelle came through from the kitchen, she had lost even more weight since Gammon found her. "How are you Michelle?" "She isn't too good, are you Michelle?". All the time Gammon was speaking to her she was twirling the end of her cardigan sleeve nervously. "Can you remember anything that might help us catch this person Michelle?" She said she had tried and tried but nothing came back. "This is a classic case of trauma related to fear Michelle. Was it a man or a woman or both?" "I remember seeing a tattoo on an arm when he or she got me round the neck" "Can you

## The Poet And The Calling Card

remember what the tattoo looked like?" "No it was a blur, I'm sorry Mr Gammon" and she broke down sobbing. "Don't worry Michelle, you have been very brave" "This fiend as killed again hasn't he Mr Gammon?" "Sadly two more times". "Michelle was so lucky Mr Gammon, I can't thank you enough" "I know it's difficult Michelle, but your memory will come back and anything you can tell me will help" "I know Mr Gammon, I am trying. I am scared he or she will come after me again." "You need not worry on that score, he won't." "Just try and get your life back. Thank you for the tea Mr Wilkinson, I will leave you in peace. Just call me Michelle, even if you think it's irrelevant." Michelle nodded and Gammon left.

Out of the three suspects he had noticed the vicar had a tattoo, Rinko Bolan had a tattoo but he wasn't sure about Rachel Fiche. The problem was tattoos were very

## The Poet And The Calling Card

common these days, so without a description it wasn't really proving anything.

Gammon was nearly home when his phone rang. "Hi John" "Sandra are you ok." "I've been feeling really rough, sorry about not making work. Mum said it will be a boy if I am this rough." This comment pulled a bit on John, like all men he wanted a boy. "Sorry to trouble you, only Mum has asked if you would like to come to the hall for Christmas dinner?". John was taken aback by this. "Why would she say that Sandra?" "Don't shout, but she knows we have been seeing each other prior to the baby shock. She was questioning me the other night and I had no choice but to tell her who the father is. I know you said not too, but I didn't want my mum thinking I slept around and she knew we had been seeing each other, so she put two and two together." "Oh I can see the problem Sandra. Have you told her

## The Poet And The Calling Card

how I feel about it?" "Yes she knows, she isn't judgemental, John. She said what will be, will be, but I thought you should know" "Can I get back to you on the Christmas dinner at the hall?" "Of course John, speak later".

The whole thing had John rethinking his actions. Suddenly the phone rang again and it was DCI Fringe. "John, can you get down to Temple Street in Derby? We have an incident occurring, quite serious." "On my way Donna, what is it?" "I will explain when you get here."

Gammon arrived at Temple Street the whole street was cordoned off, there were two ambulances, numerous police vans and cars and the Fire service. Gammon dipped under the Crime scene tape and met Donna. "What the hell is happening Donna?". "We have two officers in that pub." "What the Lord Nelson?" "Yes, they had a tip off Chi would be there tonight, so I sent DI Smarty and DI Cus'tard to sit

## The Poet And The Calling Card

and wait in the pub. About two hours ago I got a mumbled message from Cus'tard saying they had been rumbled, but then the call went dead."

"So what instigated all this action?" "We took a call from a Joe Davies, who said two men were being beaten mercilessly in the pub, he had just left. He said one of the men doing the beating was Chinese. Mr Davies then proceeded to tell me that he wasn't using his real name for fear of retribution and he hung up."

"How close have we got to the pub?" "This is it John." "Let me see what I can do." "I won't have you putting yours or my officer's lives at risk John" "Donna if we don't sort this, Smarty and Cus'tard could be killed." John left Donna looking bemused. He found a back entrance where he could hear Cus'tard pleading to stop whatever they were doing. The back of the pub was quiet, other than Sky news, coming from the bar. John picked up a

## The Poet And The Calling Card

litre bottle of Vodka and crawled to the side of the bar. The pub was empty other than a tall Chinese man, who appeared to be the aggressor, and a mountain of a man, in a full length leather trench coat, but he seemed to be just watching. It was time to make a decision, Gammon could not see any firearms but he could see the front of the Chinese guy.

With one blow from the vodka bottle he dropped the big guy, the noise made the Chinese guy turn, it was then that Gammon realised he had a gun. Gammon flung a bar stool at him, this made the gun go off, hitting Cus'tard in the shoulder. Gammon kicked out his foot pushing the back of the Chinese guys knee the wrong way, he let out a scream and dropped the gun. Gammon then hit the guy with all he had and he passed out. Making sure everything was safe he released Smarty and Cus'tard and phoned Donna to get the ambulance boys in for Cus'tard. The two

## The Poet And The Calling Card

aggressors were cuffed and loaded into a police van.

Smarty, although knocked about, wasn't as bad as Cus'tard, he thanked Gammon. "All in a day's work mate." Gammon didn't expect the dressing down he got from Donna Fringe.

"A word John, she took him into a side room. Tonight I saw the Maverick side of you John and I am not happy. You could have been killed, as could Cus'tard and Smarty. I will not have you disregarding orders again, do I make myself clear? I will decide later if I am to report this insubordination to my superiors." Gammon stood amazed at Donna's vitriolic words. "I will speak with you later Ma'am, when all this has calmed down", and Gammon left the scene.

He drove back to the Peak District calling at the Spinning Jenny to see Kev. The pub was busy it was a Young Farmers

## The Poet And The Calling Card

Christmas dinner. Joni, Kev and to John's surprise Jo Wicket's sister, Tracey Rodgers, was also working behind the bar. Tracey came to serve him. "Mr Gammon, the AWOL Detective, nice to see you again, what can I get you?" "Yeah sorry about Barcelona Tracey, flippin' work got in the way" "Only joking John." Joni was tab hanging and threw John a derisory glance.

"Can I have a pint of Pedigree please Tracey?" "Can't do love hearts on Pedigree. Only on Guinness, do you want to swap?" "I will just have to pretend then" John replied. Tracey came back she was a very bubbly character. John wasn't certain if he had done right coming to the Spinning Jenny with the amount of people in there. He sat at the bar and ordered his second pint. Sheba Filey came in with Jack and Shelley Etchings. "Hey look Shelley, it's the Sky News hero." "Now what are you talking about?" said John.

## The Poet And The Calling Card

"You have just been on Sky News, you saved those Police officer's in the Lord Nelson. It's all over the new channels." "Oh crap." "Why crap John?" "I disobeyed orders to go in, so my new boss will hang me out to dry I dare bet". "Wish we had a few more people like you in the world, John." "Appreciate that Shelley, wish the force did. What are you three drinking?" "I will have a double rum and coke please John" "Shelley?" "Just a half of Stella, please" said Shelley. "Jack?" "I'll have a pint of Stella old lad, if that's ok?" John ordered the drinks, Jack and Shelley grabbed two seats near the window leaving Sheba and John at the bar. "Looks like you are stuck with me John." "I can think of a lot worse people than a beautiful, dark haired, dusky maiden like you Sheba" "Ahh that's nice of you Mr Gammon. You should audition for the Bourne Trilogy my little action man!!" "Ok I will keep talking to you but if you drop the hero bit." Sheba laughed, "Ok but

## The Poet And The Calling Card

I'm proud of you John." "Thanks but it is a bit embarrassing to be honest." "Ok I will stop the smart arse comments. Are you stopping all night?" "I wasn't going to" said John "with it being so packed. Why, what about you?" "Well I grabbed a lift with Jack and Shelly, I was going to have some tea, but they weren't." "Would you like to go to Up The Steps Maggie's for something to eat?" "Well if you don't mind taking me and dropping me of on the way back John?" "It would be my pleasure to have a meal with a stunning gypsy girl!!". "Why do you always say I look like a gypsy?" "Ok, first you have big blue eyes, long black hair, you tend to wear big earrings and blouses off the shoulder, so you remind me of the girl in Zorro." "Not seen the film, I hope she is ok then." "Oh she is definitely ok Sheba. I think Catherine Zita Jones played her."

They arrived at the pub which was a lot quieter than the Spinning Jenny. "A pint of

## The Poet And The Calling Card

Pedigree, please, and a trio of Derbyshire sausages, with cheddar mash and vegetables please. What do you want Sheba?" "I'll have Lasagne, with crusty bread, salad and a large white wine please John."

They sat in a corner. "So how are you Sheba? Not seen much of you lately." "Happen that's a good thing John, you are such a flirt. Which woman is on the go now? I hear you took Tracey Rodgers out in Barcelona". "Let me clarify that, we only had a drink because the rest wanted to go back to the hotel." Sheba laughed "A likely story Mr Gammon. So what about Sandra? Oh and Saron?". "Nothing we're good mates and have a drink together." "Ok Mr Gammon, I can see you are giving nothing away." "So how is your love life Miss Filey." "Pretty much the same I guess?".

"Wow, look at that for food." The plates were overflowing. "I heard they had a new

## The Poet And The Calling Card

chef here" said Sheba, "Cheryl mentioned it at Badminton last week, she said the food was good."

After a lovely meal, Sheba said she was ready for home. "I have a heavy day tomorrow, this weather isn't great for farming John." "I'll bet, mind you, you look well on it." "There you go again, Flirty Gammon!!" "No, I mean it." They arrived back at Sheba's and she pecked him on the cheek. "Don't I get a nightcap then?" "Sorry cheeky, early start tomorrow, thank you for a nice evening see you soon." With that Sheba disappeared up the path and into the house.

The following morning John was up like a lark, the drive to Bixton was a little dodgy but he arrived safe and sound. "Morning Sandra" "Morning John, I think DCI Fringe wants to speak with you".

## The Poet And The Calling Card

Gammon knocked on her office door. "Come in. Have a seat John." "Look if it's about last night?" "John I have said all I am going to say on that subject. You are brave, but stupid in the same amounts. The two guys we got, one of them is cooperating completely. The other guy, the sadistic Chinese guy, is saying nothing. I want you to interview him." "I thought I was stopping on the serial killer case?" Fringe looked at him with annoyance in her eyes. "I am not asking John, I am ordering."

Gammon was annoyed and decided it was time to give Donna both barrels. "Let me tell you something Donna. I realise the pressure of the job you are doing because I have been there and have the tee shirt. Just a little tip, don't piss off your officers." Donna tried to get a word in but John was having none of it. "You are putting people into boxes which makes them feel less important and that has the effect of

## The Poet And The Calling Card

demoralising them. You are new Donna, you have to build respect and trust with them. Ok, I've had my say".

Donna looked at John. "Sorry John, I know you are correct, I can be a bit brusque at times" "Right where is this Chinese man?" "In Interview room one, with his solicitor from Derby, Arthur Garrett, quite a hardnosed character."

"Ok let me have go", John got up to go. "Thanks John." "Not a problem" and he left Donna looking out of her window.

Sergeant Milton set the tape running. "Detective Inspector Gammon", he announced. "Been demoted Mr Gammon?". These were the first words out of Arthur Garrett's mouth. "Mr Garrett, we are not here to discuss my career, more the serious position your client finds himself in today."

## The Poet And The Calling Card

"What is your name?" Gammon said to the Chinese man. "No comment." "Ok you have played this game before. I will tell you how this is going to work. Your partner in crime is singing like a bird because he realises the very serious nature of your crime. You held captive, two of Her Majesty's Police Officers, badly beating them. You had a gun which was fired, injuring one of the officers. Just for the ABH charge alone, we would push that this was taken to Crown Court. The maximum sentence you would get could be life time's two. That is before we start on related crime of holding the police officers against their will at gun point. Do you want me to go on?"

Garrett whispered in his client's ear. "My name is Ken Wax." "Your age?" "I am thirty seven years old." "Do you live in the UK legally?". Wax turned to Garrett. Wax replied he was. "Are you sure about this Mr Wax?" "Yes", he replied. "Who

## The Poet And The Calling Card

do you work for?" "I am a nightclub bouncer. I work most of the clubs in Derby you can check." "Oh we will Mr Wax. So who pays your wages?" "Whoever I work for on that night." said Wax. "Do you know Chan Chi?". Surprisingly, he said yes. "Have you worked for him?" "Yes I have." "Were you working for him in regard to the incident you are being held here for today?" "No comment." "Mr Wax, the game is up now, I can help lighten your sentence by saying you cooperated fully with our investigations, but that deal will not be on the table as long as your mate next door is beating you to it."

"Ok yes, I was working protection for him." "Was he in the pub that night?" "Yes, he was in a back room, we were told to watch the pub". "Did he say why?" "He said the police were looking for him?" "So Mr Wax, how did all this kick off?" "Mr Chi sent a message that he had seen one of

## The Poet And The Calling Card

the officers before. He was watching on the CCTV camera. He said his name was Inspector Smarty and we were to clear the pub, give them a good beating, then we could go and he would take over." "Was his plan to kill the officers?" Wax went quiet. "You are going to look after me aren't you? Chi is a nasty piece of work."

Wax was sweating and clearly very concerned for his life. "Carry on and I will do my best." "Yes, I think he was going to kill them. He had some plastic to put on the shop floor and he told us when we were done, he would do the deed, is what he said, then he said he would call us and we must dispose of the bodies."

Gammon could feel his total hatred for Chi, bubbling up. "Where is Chi now?" "He was in hiding." "Where?". "Not sure." Gammon banged his fists on the table making Wax jump, "I am not playing games, where is he?" "He has a narrow

## The Poet And The Calling Card

boat at Shelton Locks, it's called China Rose, he will be there Mr Gammon."

"Ok. Interview suspended." Garrett asked Gammon again, "You will have to keep your promise." "Not if we lock Chi up at the same time" and Gammon smiled and left Garrett swearing under his breath.

Gammon reported his findings to Donna, they quickly dispatched Rapid response Followed by donna and himself.

Shelton Lock was a serene place, there was a row of brightly coloured canal boats sitting quietly on the canal. All this was soon to be washed away if Chi got nasty.

Right in the middle of the row was the China Rose, with its decorative barge painting of roses on the side. Donna insisted on going in first for the arrest, followed by the rapid response team and Gammon was at the back. There was a lot of shouting and four shots fired. One of

# The Poet And The Calling Card

the Rapid response guys brought DCI Fringe out she was clearly shaken but ok.

"What happened Donna?" "He was in bed with a young girl when he saw me, he pulled a gun from under his pillow. Luckily, by then, two of the Rapid Response Team were through the hatch and they fired. I think one fired three shots and the other fired one, he is dead John."

John could see she was shaken, so he took his coat off and wrapped it round her, holding her tight. "Well done Donna, that's a big result for the force." "Thank you John", and she smiled. John thought how pretty she was when she smiled.

They went back to Bixton leaving the Crime Scene people to do their job. John got Donna a sweet tea to help with the shock. "I need to pull myself together John and get a report done on this." "Well if you need any help, just give me a shout." "Appreciate that, thanks John."

# The Poet And The Calling Card

Gammon was feeling quite good, the suspects in the serial killer case he did feel it was one of the three, and now the tattoo mentioned was starting to make him think that also.

Chan Chi was no longer a pain in his side and there would no longer be a drawn out court case to have to go through. He decided to go and see DI Cus'tard and DI Smarty at the hospital to tell them the good news. Just as he was leaving they both walked through the front door.

"What are you two doing out?" "Can't keep good coppers down they replied". "Well clearly you can't work DI Cus'tard." "I will be fine John, my arm is broken but everything else is just bruised, the bullet only grazed my shoulder." 'This is commitment' Gammon thought. "Well if you are both sure.". They then both thanked John Gammon. "If it hadn't have

## The Poet And The Calling Card

been for your swift action, I am sure we would have been dead John." "Hey that's fine lads, you would do the same for me, I know that."

"What time is the Christmas party on the 19th John?" "Not got a clue Dave, I just paid my money and will turn up, about 8.00pm I guess." "It's only a week away." "It only seems like two minutes ago. I know where has the time gone?" Donna Fringe was stood talking to Sergeant Yap. Donna appeared aggravated. "Morning Ma'am." "Good morning John. You haven't by any chance seen DI Scooper on your travels?" "No why?" "Well she should have been on the desk at 6.00am this morning, but she didn't show and we have just had her mother on wanting to speak to her?"

"I'll give her a call on her mobile." Gammon rang the number it rang three times then switched onto a recording of somebody laughing. By now DCI Fringe

## The Poet And The Calling Card

had gone to her office so Gammon followed her. "Listen to this Donna." "What is it John?" "I just rang Sandra's phone and after three rings I got this man laughing. The laugh sounds evil Donna."

"Something is wrong Donna, I can feel it." "She will probably turn up in a bit, maybe she had a doctor's appointment or something and didn't want to worry her Mum." Gammon wasn't sure, he headed for his office and the drudge of going through the post. It was a beautiful winter's morning the light was streaming through the office window lighting up his desk.

On top of his pile of post was an Orange envelope. He opened it and read the contents.

**"*Dear John,***

# The Poet And The Calling Card

*I know I said I would not snatch anybody else, but with it being Christmas it would be a pity to waste this opportunity that has presented itself. I will break my rule and tell you who I have, Detective Inspector Scooper, no less. Pretty girl, shame she is going to suffer. Well, when I say suffer, that really depends on your detective skills. She will stay alive until midnight, on New Year's Eve and if you have not found her by then, she will die just like the others you failed.*

*So our game begins today. Until New Year's Eve I will give you a small clue that may lead you to her. So here is number one.*

*"Wet walls covered in green slime. Good luck John, the clock is ticking."*
*The Poet"*

Gammon slumped back in his chair, this is sick person and they are making this personal now.

## The Poet And The Calling Card

Gammon headed straight for Donna Fringe. Donna was very quiet when she read the letter. "He appears to have a grudge against you John." "It seems that way Donna." "Let's check everyone released in the last year, that you have put away, and let's see if that turns up any clues."

"I can't think what he means by 'wet walls covered in green slime', I am just hoping he hasn't buried her and maybe she is being kept in a cellar." "Let's see if we have any CCTV, see if she stopped in Bixton on the way to work. That's our only hope if she was snatched on the way to Bixton". "There are no CCTV cameras in the countryside Donna."

"Right get everyone together John, we need everyone aware of what's happened. Then after the meeting you best speak with Sandra's mum."

# The Poet And The Calling Card

Donna assembled everyone in the incident room. "Ok listen up everyone, we have just received another Orange envelope. The contents have outlined that DI Sandra Scooper has been snatched and is being held against her will. We are to be given a series of clues leading up to New Year's Eve and if we don't find Sandra by then, our killer has stated he will take her life. First things first, I don't want the press boys getting hold of this, it could jeopardise Sandra's life. Here is the letter" and Donna handed it round.

There was quietness about the room. "Do we think she maybe in a cellar? Maybe near a river perhaps, Ma'am?" "Good call Sergeant Milton. Any of you who are local have any ideas?".

"There are the old corn warehouses down by the canal. Worth a look?" "Ok Milton, Smarty and Cus'tard take two dog handlers and search the warehouses and

## The Poet And The Calling Card

the cellars. If doors are locked open them. I want a thorough search. Let's get to it."

"Donna I will be at a funeral on Wednesday. My former colleagues step daughter, Stella Coles. I feel I should be there". Donna went pale, do you think I should go, seeing I was the one who opened the door?" "I don't think that is a good idea for you or her mother, Donna." "Ok, thanks John." "Listen I'd better go and see Sandra's Mum." "All the best jobs hey John?"

Gammon left Bixton, his mind really was on Sandra and the baby. All the time he was driving from Bixton, he was thinking of poor Sandra and how she was being held and how could somebody do this to a pregnant women? John pondered, was he right to have told Sandra he didn't want to be tied down with a baby? or was it time he grew up? It was no good beating himself up, he had to use the negative thoughts and turn them into positive ones

## The Poet And The Calling Card

to find Sandra before either she, or the baby, or both were killed.

John arrived at Pritwich Hall, a big Georgian Manor House. Gammon parked his car and opening the large wrought iron gates he could see Sandra's mother talking to the gamekeeper. "Mr Gammon, lovely to see you" she shouted. "Would you like tea?". John thought it best to take her inside and explain the situation. Lady Hasford ordered tea and she summoned John into the drawing room. The room was immaculate painted in a pastel blue colour on two sides with oak panelling on the other two walls. On the walls were oil paintings, of what he assumed were the Hasford families during the ages. To the front of the room were two beautiful oak doors with leaded glass that opened onto a lawn, croquet pitch and tennis courts. The room was massive. In one corner sat a Grand Piano, with silver picture frames sat majestically on top. There were three,

## The Poet And The Calling Card

triple seated, leather settees and two leather winged back chairs. John sat in one of the chairs while the maid poured the tea. "I've still not heard from my Sandra, Mr Gammon, so I am a little worried, especially with the baby etc". John felt a little uncomfortable but ploughed on. "Lady Hasford, I am afraid I have some bad news" and John proceeded to tell her of Sandra's plight. Lady Hasford stared into space, a small tear rolled down her cheek. "I am sorry to ask you this, but did Sandra see anybody last night?" "Mr Gammon, I think you know she only has eyes for you and now with the baby as well." John again shuffled in his seat. "I will find her Lady Hasford." "I hope so Mr Gammon, you owe her that much."

After a little more conversation, John told her not to utter a word, which she gave him her word she would not. "I will keep you fully up to speed Lady Hasford, please

## The Poet And The Calling Card

try not to worry, I will find Sandra I promise."

John left Pritwich Hall with every emotion running through his body. He made his way to the canal side warehousing. Gammon arrived just as the search was being called off. Sergeant Milton met him. "We have found nothing Sir." "Did you enter every building and cellar Sergeant Milton?" "Yes, we had to break down five doors and nothing was left to chance." "Bollocks" John said and walked away cursing his luck. It was 6.15pm and John did what he always did if things were going against him. He headed for the Spinning Jenny and a pint with Kev.

"Oh blimey you look down, what's up lad?" "I'll tell you Kev, but you can't breathe a word." "You know me John lad, my words my bond." "This serial killer that is still at large and he has got Sandra Scooper." "What?" "It's worse Kev." "How can it be worse?" "She is carrying

## The Poet And The Calling Card

my baby." Kev had just taken a drink of his Low C and the shock made him spray it everywhere. "Bloody hell lad that's a turn up." "Thing is Kev, I had told Sandra I would pay for the child but I didn't want to be involved, but now it's like I know I have made a mistake Kev."

"Look lad, you have had a lot of trauma these last couple of years, with your Mum and Dad, brother, your Uncle Graham and of course Vicky. You nearly died as well lad and all this will have taken it out of you. I am not saying you are right with Sandra, just that I can understand." Kev was like a dad to John and he took on all he said. "Look she is a brave girl and you are a great detective, you will find her." "I hope so Kev, the bloody clock is ticking."

"What are you drinking John?" "I'll have a pint of Pedigree and a brandy chaser." "Are you sure lad?" "One hundred percent, Kev."

## The Poet And The Calling Card

Kev had seen this many times with John, it was the way he coped with things. Doreen brought his drink over, "Budge up bugger lugs, I'm having a drink with you. I overheard what you said about Sandra being taken. I won't say anything, but if ever she needed John Gammon in the right frame of mind it's now." "I know Doreen I'm ok, I just need to get my thinking cap on. Being honest with you I am afraid he is playing with me and will kill Sandra and the baby, as there seems to be only me he wants to communicate with."

"Come on lad, be positive I am sure you will find her and this maniac." Doreen had to leave John to help in the kitchen. Carl Milton came in bought John a drink and sat with him. "Are you ok John? I know that is a daft question with Sandra and all that. Look it's none of my business but the word at the station is she is pregnant by you." John looked at Carl. "No comment." "Fine by me John, but please be aware we

## The Poet And The Calling Card

are all gutted for Sandra and any hours, even working over Christmas, the whole station would do it for nothing."
"Appreciate that Carl and I am sure Sandra will, when we find her."

They sat chatting for the rest of the night before Carl suggested he take John home, as he was a little the worse for wear.

Carl dropped John at the cottage and he went in. It was becoming customary for him to pour himself a large Jameson's whisky at times like this, which he did. The next thing John knew it was 6.00am, although it was now the weekend, he felt he wanted to go into work in case anything came up.

After a quick breakfast John arrived at the station, to his surprise all the staff were in. They had told Donna they didn't want paying. Donna met John, "We have two people you put away John, one lives in near Bixton, his name is Gavin Strop.

## The Poet And The Calling Card

Apparently you put him away for eight years, when you were in London." "I remember that little tosser, he beat his next door neighbours wife to with an inch of her life because she informed the police he was growing cannabis in his loft. Nasty little tosser. Why would he come to live near Bixton?"

"Well they have sent a car for him and the duty solicitor. The other guy is an ex copper Lee Rune." "Blimey that's a name from the past. Me, him and Whisky joined the force together on the first day. He got five years didn't he?" "That's correct John, but he vowed to get even with you and Whisky." "Yes it's all coming back to me now Donna. He was bent. Whisky caught him selling pills to school kids. Apparently Whisky never said anything the first time but then he was on a raid with him at a drug dealers place and he took a suitcase of heroin and offered Whisky a quarter of its contents. Whisky

## The Poet And The Calling Card

told me and I bubbled him. He hated me and Whisky and vowed to get even." "He got eleven years John and is out on parole and living in Ackbourne." "Why flippin' Ackbourne I wonder?" "Well we will find out he's also coming in."

First to arrive was Gavin Strop. Gammon didn't recognise him. Strop was polite and courteous. They went into interview room one. Strop stood up and offered his hand to Gammon as a greeting. Gammon noticed he had a tattoo on his arm. "It's nice to see you, Mr Gammon, after all these years. Could I just say, for the record, I am willing at any time to be questioned by the Police? I regret my past whole heartedly."

Smarty got the interview tape running. "Gavin? Is it ok if I call you Gavin?" "Yes it is Sir, how can I help you?" "You may or may not be aware Gavin but we have a serial killer at large." "Yes I am aware Sir." "The serial killer is using me

## The Poet And The Calling Card

somewhat as his communicator. We have a theory that the killer could be somebody from my past that holds a grudge against me. You fall into that category Gavin." "Mr Gammon, I was a stupid young man all those years ago, but I am a god fearing man now. I do charity work and attend church."

This made Gammon sit up, knowing the connections they were looking for, maybe Gavin had just made his first mistake. "Why have you come to live near Bixton Gavin?" "I got into the Church whilst I was in prison and when I got out I had the chance of a farming job in Wiggly, just outside Bixton. I joined the local church and have made many friends. From that I have been part of the Charity work the churches in the area arrange."

Gammon thought about asking him about dates and times but the girls were all held so the murders didn't happen on certain days that were traceable. "Would you

## The Poet And The Calling Card

mind writing your name on this piece of paper Gavin?" "Not at all Sir."

Gavin wrote 'Gavin Strop'. It was legible and not really what he thought was the same as on the poems but he still wanted it analysing.

"I am going to give you some names and I want you to tell me if you know these people?" "Ok Sir, I will do my best." "Mandy Nichol, Michelle Wilkinson, Annabelle Leaf, Stella Coles and Sandra Scooper. Do you know or have you had any contact with these people?" "I think I know the name Mandy Nichol. I do know Annie Leaf, she was on a lot of the Charity do's set up by the Church. Annie was a nice girl very sensible." "Did she have a boyfriend Gavin?" "I never saw her with anyone but to be honest we are busy when we do these Charity things Mr Gammon."

Gammon could not believe the transformation in Strop. Was it too good to

## The Poet And The Calling Card

be true? Was there maybe two people carrying out these crimes and he was an accomplice. "So you have never heard of, or had contact with, the other three girls? Have you ever had contact with anybody in the area that worked with the Church?" "I know the vicar of Pritwich, Matt Spouncer, what a great guy he is so dedicated." "When you say you know Mr Spouncer, how well do you know him?" "I don't know if I should say this but I am gay Mr Gammon, and so is Matt, but he hasn't come out yet. He invited me down for a long weekend some time back. Nothing untoward just that he was struggling with his sexuality and he needed to talk to someone."

'The mind boggles', Gammon thought Spouncer didn't seem camp or gay but you never know he thought.

"We've stayed good friends ever since but he will only be at peace with himself when he accepts who he is." Something was

## The Poet And The Calling Card

bugging Gammon but he had little he could pin on Strop. "Well it's good to see you have turned your life round Gavin, we will be in touch should we need to speak further." "Anytime Mr Gammon" and Gavin thanked him and left. "Well that was a waste of time Dave" "Looks that way John, he seemed like a nice guy." "Certainly was a different man to the one I put away."

"Right let's see Lee Rune next door." Rune had decided he wanted his own solicitor and had brought along Tony Brinyard. Brinyard was an Ackbourne solicitor who dealt with most of the local pond life, he was a big, imposing man, almost six feet four and about seventeen stone. He didn't like the police and they didn't like him. His method's had secured many non-conviction's for his low life clients. Gammon knew this was going to be challenging.

## The Poet And The Calling Card

Milton had set the tape up when Gammon and Smarty entered the room. "Well if it isn't Old Snitch Gammon, the Serpico of the Met." "Good afternoon Lee." "I never thought I would see you again, Gammon, you or your poxy mate. I hear he got himself shot but survived, more is the pity." Rune's solicitor leaned forward telling Rune to calm down.

Rune was having none of it. "What's it like to rat on a fellow officer, hey Gammon? Not only did I go down for five years, but I lost my wife, kids, house and career, all because of the righteous John bloody Gammon."

"If you have quite finished Lee, I would like to ask you some questions. Why have you moved to Ackbourne?" "None of your business, you're a detective, you work it out." Smarty dived in. "You said at your trial you would get even with DI Gammon and DI Grant. What did you mean by that?" "No comment." "I will give you

## The Poet And The Calling Card

five names, I want to know if you know any of these girls. Mandy Nichol?" "No comment" "Michelle Wilkinson?" "No comment" "Annabelle Leaf?" "No comment" "Stella Coles?" "No comment" "Sandra Scooper?"

At this name, Rune started to laugh. "What? He has taken a copper? Top-man. Making you look stupid Gammon." Gammon lost it and DI Smarty had to restrain Gammon. "Hit a nerve hey Gammon?", and Rune laughed again. "If you have anything to do with any of the abductions or the killings of these girls, I will get you Rune, make no mistake." "Followed your career Gammon, you are in the last chance saloon, just been demoted I hear. The great John Gammon fall's on his arse again." "Interview terminated" Gammon retorted. "You have not heard the last from me Rune. You make one mistake and I will be there to

## The Poet And The Calling Card

send you back to where you belong, away from society."

At this Rune lost it. "I will never go back inside, I am scarred because of you Gammon. Do you know what they do to ex coppers inside?". Rune's solicitor pulled him away still ranting as they left the station.

Smarty was concerned. It wasn't like Gammon to lose control. "Are you ok John? Look mate you have been a good gaffer to me and now we are on the same level it seems strange, but one things for sure, you have the total respect of the station. So if you need to talk, it won't go any further". Gammon sat back down with only Dave Smarty and himself in the room he opened up to DI Smarty. "I guessed as much John. Sandra doesn't play around and we knew you had been seeing her, so you don't have to be a rocket scientist to put two and two together." "I'm gutted Dave, this maniac not only has Sandra, he

## The Poet And The Calling Card

also has my baby. I think he is playing with me and I think he will kill Sandra for sure. I am wondering if these clues actually mean anything or are they just trying to move us off the scent?"

"We will find her John, she is one of us." "I hope so Dave, I really do." Gammon called at Donna's office on the way to his and went through what happened in the two interviews. "It appears that he still holds a grudge" "John, I am going to assign a PC to watch him twenty-four-seven." "Good idea Donna, he is twisted enough to be doing this."

Gammon left Donna and headed to his office. He froze when he saw another Orange envelope in his mail. Ignoring everything else he opened it.

**"Hi John,**

*With Scooper safe and suffering, I thought I would test your abilities. You*

## The Poet And The Calling Card

*will get another clue on Thursday, but before then I could not resist nicking another one.*

*She will die by my timing at midnight on Christmas Day, thought I would bring it forward as a kind of Christmas present for you. That is of course if you don't find her first. I told you at the beginning I would do seven, but I have decided to do six. Scooper being my last entertainment. That way I can save one for another day, I'm not greedy you know. Anyway here goes the clue to the little lady I have in my custody.*

*This one I will cut up into a small piece, to keep her secret from the police.*

*At midnight on Christmas Day she will meet her demise. Let's hope she has been baptized.*

*The reason I do this is plain to see to save this girl look for the Golden Key.*

# The Poet And The Calling Card

*Happy Christmas John, Tick Tock*

*The Poet."*

John felt sick to his stomach, he knew with current resources and with having only until midnight Christmas Day for Sandra to survive, efforts would have to be increased.

He hurried to Donna's office and showed her the latest offering from The Poet.

Donna confirmed that they would change priorities and find this poor girl. "Get something on the missing persons register". No sooner had Donna spoken when Sergeant Yap knocked on the door. "Sir I have a Jack Etchings in reception, he seemed quite upset, he wants to speak to you." Gammon went downstairs. "Hello mate." Jack could hardly get his words. "What's the matter?" "It's Shelley, she hasn't come home since last night". "What time was this Jack? She left home at

# The Poet And The Calling Card

6.30pm to play badminton with Sheba and Cheryl". "Did she get there?" "No the girls said they waited but she didn't turn up. I have been out all night looking for her. I tried ringing her mobile but it's switched off. I phoned everyone I could think of and all the local hospitals, but nothing. Just checked with your desk sergeant and nobody has reported an accident. It's like she has been abducted by aliens, John." "Get Jack a strong sweet coffee please, Carl." Milton went off to sort it. "Let's take a statement Jack, so we know what she was wearing etc."

John started to write. "So she left Ardwalk at 6.30pm heading for Pritwich Village Hall?" "Yes John". "What was she wearing?" "She had on some black Adidas track suit bottoms, and a white tee shirt with a collar, she always wore that she, said she played better in it. She had on white trainers with a green flash up the side". "Ok did she have a bag?" "Yes, a

## The Poet And The Calling Card

brown leather holdall I bought for her birthday. She had her clothes to change into in there." "What clothes were they Jack?" "I don't know John, she packed the bag whilst I wasn't there."

"Ok, which car was she driving?" "She went in the silver BMW registration number SHE 11Y, you know Shelley". "Ok that should be easy to trace Jack. Sorry to have to ask you this Jack but have you two been getting on ok?" "Yes, of course John, hardly had a cross word in thirty five years of marriage." "I know that mate but I have to ask". "John, the only night Shelley goes out without me is either to badminton with the girls or once a year for the horticultural show that she does with Sheba Filey and Cheryl, and I always meet her at the pub afterwards." "Can you think of anything else that might be important?" Jack waited a second then he said, "Last weekend we went to see the vicar, Shelley wanted to renew our vows."

## The Poet And The Calling Card

"Which church Jack?" "Hittington." "Who is the vicar there?" "Reverend Spouncer John, why?" "I thought he was the vicar at Pritwich?" "They only have one now John, he does Cowdale as well I think. He is a really nice guy, he enthused about our wanting to renew our vows and said he would get back to us with a date."

"Anything else Jack?" "I can't think of anything." "So Shelley wasn't depressed or anything." "No, blimey you know Shelley, life and soul of the party John, not a lot gets Shelley down." "Ok mate we will get looking for her, I can't officially send out a search party as she isn't a minor, but I personally will retrace her journey to see if I can see anything. I'm sure something will turn up mate" and John put his hand on Jack's shoulder to reassure him.

It was almost 7.30pm when John left the station, no further forward on finding Sandra and now Shelley had gone walk

## The Poet And The Calling Card

about. He decide to go home get the tea that Phyllis Swan, his cleaner, would have left out for him. She cooked most weeks on the pretence she had over-made and she didn't want it going to waste, but he knew she made him a meal because she thought he didn't look after himself.

John arrived at the farm and the cottage at 8.05pm. He got his keys out of his pocket and went to open the door but the door wasn't locked. He assumed Phyllis must have stayed late cleaning. "Hello Phyllis, are you here?". No reply, he switched the lights on and on the table was an Orange envelope. Next to it was a note from Phyllis. "John I have left you a Lasagne in the microwave and there is a salad in the fridge and some garlic bread in the oven. I will lock up and leave the key under the flowerpot, usual place. See you next week.

Phyllis x

# The Poet And The Calling Card

John went to the flowerpot sure enough the keys were there. Perhaps she had thought she had locked up. Next he opened the Orange envelope.

**Dear John,**

*Nice lady that cleaner, if I had not decided to just do six snatches, she would have been ideal but maybe next time. A bit careless for a police officer to leave his keys lying about, hey John? Thought I would deliver this in person, it adds to the fun. Well it's time you tried to guess the name of this victim, so here we go.*

*Her first name is found on a beach, her surname is like engraving, thought that was a good choice with grave being in it.*

John knew instantly he had Shelley Etchings. He phoned Donna and explained everything too her. "Ok John I will get a search party out, I think we need to go to the media on this one now." "Just give it a

## The Poet And The Calling Card

couple of days please Donna, I might be wrong." "You know you are not and we only have until midnight Christmas Day, John." "I know, just two days, please Donna?" "Ok your call they are your friends". "Thanks Donna."

John poured himself a Jamesons, he didn't feel like a lasagne, knowing Sandra and Shelley were under the fear of death and this nutter had been in his house.

John sat thinking. Why would he come to his house? This was pure arrogance and John felt he must be local. What does the Golden Key mean, where would a Golden Key be?

John racked his brains for four hours but couldn't think of anything that might lead to a place where Shelley was being kept. Why would the killer talk about chopping her up to a small piece to keep her secret from the Police?

# The Poet And The Calling Card

It was 1.40am when John finally gave up. He could hardly keep his eyes open as he climbed the stairs. John brushed his teeth, he was too tired to shower so would do that in the morning. He flicked on the light in his bedroom and was taken back. The whole of the head board to his bed, was plastered in cuttings from his early police days. Above the bed head, scratched in the plaster, were the words 'John Gammon, the forces best, Ha, Ha, Ha.'.

John decided he didn't want forensics crawling all over his house so he slept in the spare room. The following morning he told Donna what had happened and the clue about the key and waited for John Walvin and his Forensic team to arrive.

With his cottage full of Police and forensics, John left for Bixton, on his way, he decided to call in and see Jack Etchings in Ardwalk. John wasn't sure about what to say, but knew he could not leave his

# The Poet And The Calling Card

friend to hear of the situation from anyone else.

Jack and Shelly had been farmers but had decided to renovate some barns for holiday accommodation. John pulled into the yard and was met by Kelly Fold, one of the housekeepers. Kelly was employed to run the accommodation. John and Kelly had been at school together. "Well long time no see John, how are you?" "Pretty good Kelly, what about you?" "Not living the exciting life you are, but still making my way in life." Kelly lived in the village and had done all her life her Mum and Dad had run the Ardwalk post office for about forty years but because of the last recession they closed it and converted it into a big house. Kelly lived next door with Chris Fold, a local joiner and general builder.

"You and Chris still an item?" "Yes we've been together almost eighteen years." "Are you married Kelly?" "No, Chris is that laid

## The Poet And The Calling Card

back I don't think it has ever entered his head to ask me" and she laughed. "We are good though John. What about you?" "Are you still with…?" There was a pause then she remembered Lindsay's name. "No, we split a few years ago" "So who is the lucky lady now then?" "Nobody Kelly, I don't have that much time to be honest with work." "So what are you doing here then?" "Just popping into see Jack." "He seems a bit distant this morning John, I think Shelley must have gone away for a few days and you know how you men can't cope" and she laughed. "Anyway I best get on, we are fully booked from now until the New Year. Nice to have seen you John." "Likewise Kelly, look after yourself."

John knocked on Jacks cottage door, the scenery around his cottage was incredible, the view on a clear day was something from a tourist calendar. "Good morning Jack." "Hi John, you heard anything?"

# The Poet And The Calling Card

"Listen mate sit down" "What is it John? She is ok isn't she?" "It's complicated Jack. We have reason to believe that Shelley is being held against her will by the man we are hunting for the serial killings." Jack went pale. "I can't lose her John she is my world."

"I didn't want this getting out and you not being fully aware. The only clue I have is, the perpetrator mentions a golden key, does that mean anything to you Jack?" Jack went silent. "Jack are you ok?"

"Many years ago Shelley told me a story about an ancestor who was a locksmith and legend has it that passed down from generation to generation, was speak of a Golden Key and that this ancestor had it made for a coffin. The coffin wasn't for a body, but for gold and jewellery that Elisabeth 1$^{st}$ buccaneers had stolen and had told Shelley's ancestor to hide in a coffin and to make a golden key, which he was the only person to hold the key. They

## The Poet And The Calling Card

told him they would be back for their booty. The legend goes onto say that they never returned. The coffin and the key are supposedly hidden somewhere in the Peak District but the old locksmith was too frightened to tell anyone where he had hidden the coffin and the key and he took the secret to his grave. It must be Shelley he has then John?" "It's certainly pointing to that Jack."

"People have looked for this forever, we quite often have people staying at the holiday accommodation, asking Shelley about the legend. In fact we had somebody only three week back." "What was his name Jack?". "Let me get the booking John. There you go Leonard Ian Andrew Riddle. I remember him because he insisted we wrote his full name." "What did he look like?" "He was a big man, overweight and a bit scruffy. His address is 1 Vineyard Terrace, Derby." "Did he

# The Poet And The Calling Card

leave a phone number?" "No it's rare they do John."

"Ok Jack sit tight, we are doing everything we can mate. I best go and check this address out."

On the way to Derby, Gammon called DI Smarty. "Dave its John, can you do me a favour mate?" "If I can John, what is it?" "Can you interview Stella Coles' best friend? Her name is Mary Bloom, but she likes to be called Mickey, she lives at The Vicarage in Smidgley on Twain its near Rotherham." "Ok John will catch up with you later." Smarty cancelled the call and Gammon carried onto Derby. He finally found Vineyard Terrace but there were warehouses on the site no houses. At the top of the street was the Vineyard pub so Gammon decided to see if any locals or the landlord might know where number one was.

# The Poet And The Calling Card

The pub was a typical, pre-war pub, window's hadn't been cleaned in years, it looked like it had been upgraded in the 1960's, but the mock leather seating was ripped and somebody had carved their name in the wooden tables. The landlord was clearly a drinker, it was early afternoon and he had a pint in his hand. Gammon showed him his warrant card. "Are you local Mr?" "Bestwood, Jim Bestwood. Yes ran this pub for thirty five years and my dad ran it for forty years before me. How can I help you Detective?"

"I have been looking for Number one Vineyard Terrace?" "Well Number one was knocked down in 1973 with the rest of the row." "Did you know who lived there?" "Yes, a Mr and Mrs Wallace. They had three girls Peggy, Dina and Joyce and a son, but he was with Mrs Wallace's first husband. He was a bit of an odd kid, think he became a vicar or one of your lot I

## The Poet And The Calling Card

can't remember." "Please try Mr Bestwood it's important." "Hey Billy, what was that little tosser that lived at Number One Vineyard Terrace called?" "Lee Wallace." "No Billy, she had him before she met Johnny Wallace, they had three girls together." "Yer right lad, I can't remember. Oh hang on. Lee Rune". "You bloody old fool, I got it now it was Rune, Lee Rune right little tosser when he were younger. They could never prove it but he slapped a lass round in Derby Park one night. She was too frightened to say who it was but we were all sure it was him. Never seen him for years but that was him."

Gammon thanked the landlord and left once in his car he phoned Donna and told her what he had found out, it was all fitting together, the name he had used at Jack and Shelley's place Leonard Ian Andrew Riddle the first and the last letter LR, Lee Rune and Riddle being the name he used to see if I could work it out,

## The Poet And The Calling Card

arrogant bastard. "Get him in Donna, I am on my way."

Gammon was feeling good about himself after all these years this little gob shite had come back to haunt him. Gammon arrived at Bixton at the same time as Rune and his solicitor. "Now what do you want? Super Cop". Rune shouted. "Put them in interview room one please Sergeant." "I will come in on this one John." "What don't you trust me Donna?" "Don't be silly, but you are emotionally attached to these last two victims."

Milton set the tape recording. "Before we go any further Mr Gammon I would like, for the tape, to state my client has cooperated with this investigation completely, but I will not allow my client to be subjected to police harassment in the future." "Have you quite finished?" Gammon said and he stared straight at Rune. "Ok Lee where were you on the following dates? December 14$^{th}$,15$^{th}$ and

## The Poet And The Calling Card

16th." "Let me see now, if I remember correctly I was in Barbados lying on a beach with Amy Winehouse before we set off on our luxury yacht, why do you ask?" Gammon lost it and had to be restrained by Milton and Fringe.

"Are you mad at me Super-cop? Why would that be?" "We know you have two women somewhere and your silly games is up". "I have women everywhere, are you short old mate?"

This time Gammon totally lost it and had to be taken out of the room. "Bloody hell John, what are you doing? You can't behave like this." "Donna, Sandra and Shelley are dying somewhere out there and that prick thinks it's funny." "You are not going back in, Smarty you come in with me, I will take the interview and John, I will see you after we have finished." John paced up and down looking through the two way glass at Rune.

# The Poet And The Calling Card

Milton stated that DCI Fringe was now conducting the interview. "My you are a pretty bit of skirt, we never had such pretty DCI's when I was in the force." "Mr Rune, would you answer the question stated by my colleague without the bullshit please?" "Seeing that you are tidy, I was in my flat in Ackbourne, only just got over the flu yesterday." "So you are saying you were laid up in your flat for the last three days?" "Correct". "Can anybody vouch for you?" "No, I live on my own since Gammon ruined my life." "What you never saw the milkman or postman?" "Just told you, I was poorly and was in bed most of the time." "Ok just to clarify, you have no witness to say you were in your flat on those days?" "That's correct". "Did you once live at number one Vineyard Terrace Derby?" "Yes I did" "Do you have any second or third names?" "None that I am aware of" "So you are not called Leonard Andrew Ian Rune?" "Nope, just Lee Rune M 'lady" "You can cut the sarcasm now

# The Poet And The Calling Card

Lee. I believe as a young man you were spoken too about an incident regarding a young woman in a park in Derby" "Look I never touched her, she never said I did, it was just the bloody neighbours stirring shit that's why I eventually went to London" "But now you are back, hey Lee?" "Is there a crime against living where I want?" "No Lee, no crime. Ok well thank you for your time and for clearing up a few points". Rune left and smirked at Gammon as he went passed. "See you soon Robocop." Fringe was behind Rune and she put her finger to her lips to indicate to Gammon not to say anything.

"Smarty organise round the clock surveillance on Rune." "Yes Ma'am" "DI Gammon my office". John followed Donna up the stairs to her office. "What the bloody hell do you think you are doing?" "He is guilty Donna, you know it and I know it and we are running out of

## The Poet And The Calling Card

time fast." "I told you this was too close a case for you. I think it would be best for you and for the case if you took some time off." "You're having a bloody laugh and leave Sandra and Shelley to the mercy of Rune? Do you not think he doesn't know we are going to be watching him, he is an ex copper, he knows all the angles Donna." "Ok John, but one more outburst like that today and you are off the case do I make myself clear?" "Yes" and Gammon stormed out of her office.

On his desk was another Orange envelope, he read the message.

*"Hi John,*

*Hope you liked the art work I left you. Well now I have two of your beauties to keep alive until I decide the end. I suppose I should give you a fighting chance.*

# The Poet And The Calling Card

***Now you know about the Golden Key, think out of the box so to speak, incidentally Shelley can't"*** and he'd put a smiley face.

***"Where would you put a coffin, in the ground perhaps, at a chapel of rest perhaps or a crematorium? And what about the Golden Key what significance is that.***

***The clocking is ticking Tick Tock John"***

***PS. I will be back to you tomorrow. Scooper is crying a lot John, not like a copper hey?"***.

Gammon decided he was keeping this to himself and was going to try and crack this case himself. But first he phoned down to Forensics. "Wally?" "Yes John" "Any luck on my place?" "Sorry John, this guy is professional, he really is" "Ok Wally, well if anything turns up let me know" "I will John".

# The Poet And The Calling Card

There was a knock on Gammon's office door so he quickly folded the note and put it in his pocket. "Come in". It was Di Trimble. "I realise this is a bad time for everyone Sir, but it's the Christmas Party at the Spinning Jenny tomorrow night and Doreen wants me to confirm numbers, will everyone be going?" "I would say yes Di, we have to keep our chin's up." "Thank you Sir" and she left. Gammon realised it was also Stella Coles funeral in the morning, which he felt he had to attend.

John called it a night with thoughts that they may have a good chance of finding Shelley and Sandra alive.

It was a clear crisp night the Derbyshire Peak District sky always threw up something new. The road to the Tow'd Man left John in awe every-time he drove there. Hittington Church steeple rose majestically above the rolling hills, it was always lit up at this time of year. People paid so much for each night to remember

## The Poet And The Calling Card

loved ones who had died and been buried there. As he rounded the corner to start rising up the hill to the Tow'd Man, a large dog fox ran in front of the Freelander. John was always aware of this as it had happened many times over the year. The fox jumped onto the limestone wall and stared at John as he went past, as much as to say 'be more careful when you are driving.' He finally arrived, the pub was quite busy there was a small party of local farmers wives, out for their Christmas meal. Angelina was on the bar as was another man, who John had never seen before.

"Hi John what can I get you?" "I'll have a pint of Risky O'Toole please Angelina. How are you?" "Good thanks John." She beckoned the new bar man over, "John this is Michael Miggs, he is from Australia and he is travelling around the UK and Europe on a gap year." John put out his hand to shake Michael's hand. "Pleased to

## The Poet And The Calling Card

meet you Michael, John Gammon" "Good to meet you John, call me Miggsy, everyone else does back home" "Ok nice to me meet you Miggsy."

"So how's John then?" "Not good Angelina." "Why what's the problem?" "This psycho killer we have loose in the Peak District, has taken Sandra Scooper and Shelley Etchings. I have until midnight Christmas Day to find Sandra or he kills her and midnight New Year's Eve to find Shelley or she has the same fate". "Any ideas? Michael, just watch the bar please. Let's sit over here." "I think it's somebody I may have put away and has a grudge. He is leaving my business cards at the scene and now he has taken Sandra and Shelley. He sends me poems and riddles, but I think this time he is deliberately making sure I am on the wrong track. A detective I worked with in London called Lee Rune, it's a long story but he hates my guts. I think he has got

## The Poet And The Calling Card

something to do with it. We have him under twenty four hour surveillance, but he is an ex copper and will know that. I didn't want that, but DCI Fringe insisted, I am concerned wherever he is holding Sandra and Shelley he won't go near them now, which means they won't get food and drink. It's just horrendous." "What sort of clues have you had?" "They are just stupid. I mean all I have for a clue is a coffin and a Golden Key. What the hell do I do with that?". Angelina agreed it was a weak clue. John had one more drink then left for home.

It's now December 19$^{th}$ the day of the funeral for Stella Coles, and the evening Christmas Party for Bixton station, John wasn't relishing either.

He arrived at the funeral of Stella Coles and sat in a pew. The coffin arrived. Matthew Spouncer, the Pritwich vicar who John still suspected, asked the congregation to stand. There was only

# The Poet And The Calling Card

about fifteen people in attendance, John thought this was low for such a young girl.

Whisky was supporting his wife, she was sobbing. 'Dreadful times' John thought and poor Whisky after all he had gone through, some people just don't get luck in life he thought.

The part pf the service that would stick forever in Gammons mind, was the strength shown by Whisky's wife, when she stood up and spoke. She had nothing written down it was all from the heart.

"Today I have lost my little girl forever, or so the person that has done this will think. But you know what, deep down my little girl believed and now she will be with her father, a God fearing man, who will take good care of my little girl. So if you are ever caught for the terrible crime you have committed, be sure that I forgive you and feel sorry for you, but your maker may not feel the same on the day you are judged

## The Poet And The Calling Card

for your wrong doings". She stood down from the pulpit. The congregation held in silence and respect for a lovely lady.

With the service over John, gave his condolences to Whisky's wife and left to go back to the station.

On Gammons mind was the coffin and the golden key. He decided to go and see an old school friend, Martyn Wright, who was a lecturer at Derby University on Peak District history. John wanted to see if he could shed any light on the Golden Key. Martyn and his wife ran a small tea shop in Hittington called Pasteles Felices. His wife actually ran it, but Martyn only worked three days a week at the University, so Gammon was hoping he would be there. Gammon pulled up outside the tea shop, it was very quaint, painted green on the outside with net curtains tied back on the big picture window. Inside there were pictures of Spain everywhere, hence the name of the

# The Poet And The Calling Card

café which meant "Happy Cakes" in Spanish. Luckily Martyn was serving.

"Hey John, lovely to see you stopping by for one of our Spanish coffees, my friend" "Well of course Martyn, but I would also like to pick your brains, if I may" "Well we can try mate, there isn't a lot of brain to pick, I'm on wind down. We are selling in two years and going to live in Spain". "Good on yer Martyn, good luck to you and your family".

Martyn brought over a strong black Spanish coffee and a homemade Tarta De Santiago with clotted cream. "Try this John, my wife's mother used to make this when she was a child and the recipe has been handed down". "What is it Martyn?" "Spanish Almond cake John" "Wow that is really good".

"Anyway mate how can I help you?" "What can you tell me about the Coffin and the Golden Key if anything?" "Oh the

## The Poet And The Calling Card

famous legend of the Buccaneers and their booty, locked in a coffin and the Golden Key given to the village locksmith. They never returned and the locksmith had given his word he would tell no one, so he went to his grave being the only person knowing where the Golden Key was. I have done research on this and the locksmith did exist over many years after he died. A Buccaneer, believed to be one of the men who gave him the key, came back and was so angry that the locksmith had died, he tortured his wife and children to get them to tell him where the coffin and the golden key was, but of course they didn't know. They apparently endured horrific days of torture before being murdered, but legend has it that one son who had been out poaching, was not at the house at the time and he left the village but was never traced. So by the writings of the time, it is quite feasible that the Coffin and the Golden Key did exist." "How you could find it though?" asked John. "I

## The Poet And The Calling Card

would not have a clue many have tried John. Why did you want to know?" "It's a long story Martyn, I won't bore you with it. Thanks for the lovely cake and coffee mate I will pop by and see you again soon" "I am usually here on Thursday's and Friday's" "Ok mate will see you soon." Gammon headed back to Bixton station.

He was met by Sergeant Yap. "It should be a good night tonight Sir, I hear The Spinning Jenny have got Abigail and the Rock Chicks, an all-girl band who do eighties music, like Susie and the Banshees stuff." Gammon smiled he didn't want to be a party pooper, but how could he settle knowing Sandra and the baby and Shelley may not be even being fed?

DCI fringe called him to her office. "Rune hasn't left his flat since being released from the interview" "Are you sure about that Donna?" "Well if you mean do I trust

## The Poet And The Calling Card

my men to do a proper job watching him then, yes."

"Rune is an ex copper and as much as I don't like him, before he went native, he was a decent copper. He will know you would be watching him. We may even have two scenarios here." "What are they John?" "Well he could still be getting out without us knowing or you are correct and he hasn't gone out, which in that case if he is our killer, then we have two victims not being fed and watered if indeed they are alive!!" Donna went quiet. "You think I have done this all wrong don't you?" "Look Donna, in your job you have to make decisions. Would I have done it differently to be honest, yes, but it wasn't my call."

"Look do you think I should pull the surveillance off then?" "I would" "Ok John, I will do it now" "Ok well I am calling it a day and will see you tonight at

## The Poet And The Calling Card

the party Donna." "Ok John and thanks for the advice."

Gammon left and headed home. Again when he opened his kitchen door there was another Orange envelope. John opened it.

*"Hello John,*

*Not doing very well with the clues. My first victim only has six days to go, you really must try harder John.*

*Noticed you have a lot of policeman doing overtime on surveillance, I hope the budget isn't being stretched too much.*

*I have another clue for you, are you ready? Singapore Chow Mein, do you like it?*

*By for now John, Tick Tock*

*The Poet"*

## The Poet And The Calling Card

What the hell does that mean John thought? He quickly showered and changed, as he was running late, and headed for The Spinning Jenny. By the time John arrived most people were there. DI Smarty brought John a pint over. "How did you go on with Mickey, Stella Coles mate Dave?" "Strange girl John, she didn't really add much, other than she did say that Stella felt freaked out by Matthew Spouncer. Apparently on a couple of the trips abroad, before her father died, he would come to her tent at night with hot chocolate and biscuits. She said he did try to touch her once but she said Stella was a bit of a fruit cake and she always found Spouncer ok."

"It has to be Rune, Dave." "I know, but what proof do we have?" "Absolutely nothing." "I know tonight will be hard for you John, with Sandra and Shelley Etchings still being held, but there is nothing you can do, and you know the

## The Poet And The Calling Card

whole team see's you as the boss" "I know Dave, I will do my best."

A surprise for the night was Angelina and Saron had booked tickets. "Hey what are you two doing here, have you shut up shop?" "No Michael and his girlfriend Debbie are running it tonight. We had no guests booked in, so thought we would have a night out and a dance before the crazy Christmas period really takes off." "What are you drinking?"

John went to the bar and ordered a double Bacardi and Coke and a double Gin and Soda. "There you go girls" "Thanks John" "How are you Dave?" "Good thanks Saron." "No wife tonight?" "No she likes that Celebrity Big Brother and the soaps, so she sit's watching them all Friday night." "Right, I am having a dance with you later." "Look forward to it Saron." The girls left John and Dave and went off dancing.

# The Poet And The Calling Card

"Look, I know you don't want to talk shop tonight Dave, but being honest with you I haven't told everyone everything." "What do you mean?" "Well, one of the clues he sent me was for Shelley, well two clues actually. One was a coffin and a Golden Key." "I read about that legend only the other night. What was the other one John?" "Don't laugh, Singapore Chow Mein."

"Just a minute John, there is Funeral Directors in Ackbourne that just closed down, something to do with the owner dying and leaving no family, so it's shut up now." "Sorry Dave, struggling to understand what you mean?" "Well, it said, that this guy had worked for a local undertakers, for almost thirty years. When the Chinese in Ackbourne shut, he converted it into a Funeral parlour." "What was the name of the Chinese Dave?" "Don't think they said."

# The Poet And The Calling Card

"Carol, Carol, come here." "Hello my little sexy copper." "Ackbourne" said John. "Yeah, what about it?". "What's the name of the Chinese Take Away?" "The Secret Garden I think." "Damn, it's not that then." Carol carried on "I never used that one, I used to love the other one before it shut. My kids used to call it. "Golkey" when they were little. They couldn't pronounce Golden Key."

John almost spit his beer over Carol. "Steady John". He gave her a big kiss and said "You are a star, come on Dave." "Where we going?". "I will tell you on the way Dave, if my hunch is correct."

Within twenty minutes they had parked in the market place close to the funeral parlour of Malcolm Graham. "Get the torch out of the glove box Dave. Listen to me, don't try and open any doors unless I say."

## The Poet And The Calling Card

The Funeral parlour looked eerie against the full moon of the night. "Come on round the back." John shone his torch into the back of the shop, he couldn't see anything just an old counter. "What's that John?" "Don't know, it says Chapel of Rest."

The chapel was a long building with a curved tin roof. It had a door to the front and a side entrance, both John and Smarty noticed what looked like a brand new lock on the door. John again shone his torch up and down but could see nothing.

"Come on, we are going in." "Do you think Shelley Etchings is being kept here?" "That's what I am hoping Dave."

They broke the lock off the side door and went in. The place smelt of death they both commented. It seemed totally empty, covered in cobwebs with a large oriental type rug covering a large amount of flooring. "She isn't here John, it doesn't

## The Poet And The Calling Card

look like anyone has been in here." "Come on detective this mat has been moved, look at the dust, then no dust where it hasn't been put back in the same place. Give me a hand Dave, let's roll it back". They rolled back the carpet and it revealed a trap door. "There must be a cellar John."

Gammon and Smarty lifted the trap door. Gammon shone his torch once more. "She's here, don't move Shelley." John could see the wire glistening as he shone the torch. "One false move and the wire will cut you." Shelley's feet were tied together, her hands were tied behind her back and she seemed to be drifting in out of consciousness. "Dave, carefully release that wire." Dave managed to do it while John held Shelley's head so she didn't go forward onto the wire. Dave undid her hands and John undid her legs. She fell into John's arms. "Dave call an ambulance urgently." Within ten minutes Paramedics had arrived and stabilised Shelley and

## The Poet And The Calling Card

whisked her off to hospital. "Come on John this deserves a beer." "Just let me phone Jack." said John.

John spoke with an elated Jack. "Thank you so much John, how will we ever repay you?" "All part of the job Jack."

Dave and John headed back to the Spinning Jenny. John made a bee line for Donna. "We have found her". John was so excited, he realised he had not told Donna everything. "Good work John, but you really have to stop being a Maverick, you are a great cop but it isn't how things are done these days". Donna turned to DI Smarty "Well done to you too Dave." "John was the brains Ma'am." "Donna please, when we are out." "Ok thanks Donna" smiled Dave.

"Are you dancing John?" "Just want a quick word with Kev, Sheba, I'll dance to the next one". "Ok Mr, spoilt for choice?"

## The Poet And The Calling Card

and she laughed and walked away. John beckoned Kev.

"We have found Shelley mate." "Is she ok John?" "She will be fine, she is a bit dehydrated, so I am guessing a couple of days in hospital." "Oh mate well done, I knew you would find her. What about Sandra?" "Nothing yet Kev." "You will find her as too, there isn't a better detective in the whole of the UK." "Thanks old mate, but I think you are biased" and he laughed.

John left Kev chuckling, as we went back to the bar. It was 11.00pm, with the party in full swing. Donna got on the stage. "Ladies and Gentlemen, colleagues, if we needed to celebrate then we have an excuse tonight. DI John Gammon and DI Dave Smarty have tonight found the sixth victim of the maniac threatening our communities here in the Peak District. Shelley Etchings has been found alive and well. She will be kept in hospital for a

## The Poet And The Calling Card

couple of days for tests but she is doing fine. So please put your hands together for two of our fantastic team, DI Gammon and DI Smarty. Thank you." Everyone was clapping and congratulating John and Dave. Dave whispered in John's ear, "I'm a bit embarrassed, don't know about you?" "Just a bit, Dave"

"This is my dance Mr Gammon". Saron grabbed John's arm, Angelina grabbed Dave Smarty's arm. Already on the dance floor Joni was dancing with Carl and Sheba was dancing with Ian Yap. Before long everyone was up in a circle dancing to 'Come on Eileen' by the Dexy's Midnight Runners. A few dances later and the group announced the last song for the night, which would be Drive, by The Cars. Saron looked longingly at John "Does this mean you are taking me home tonight John?" "If you want, I guess?" "You don't sound too happy about it Gammon." "Sorry, I have a lot on my plate at the

## The Poet And The Calling Card

moment". "Only joking, I will nip and get a taxi. Angelina is staying here tonight and it looks like Smarty has pulled." "Don't say that, his missus will kill him" "Nothing to do with me I am going home with the man I want to go home with."

Once back at the Tow'd Man Saron, poured them both a large brandy. "Who organised the official photographer? We will be all over the Derbyshire Police magazine." "I don't know, I assumed Donna did" replied John.

They both sat sipping their Brandy, Saron kicked off her shoes and lay on the settee, with her legs on John's lap. He was thinking how nice this was with Saron, but he still could not get Sandra's plight out of his mind. Was this the right time to tell Saron? He looked at Saron, she had the body of a goddess and the looks of a film star. Was he going to chance telling her?

## The Poet And The Calling Card

John knew it was now or never. "Saron I have something to tell you". "What have you done now?" "It's Sandra, she's pregnant." Saron immediately took her legs off John. "What do you mean she's pregnant? Is it yours?" "I believe so" "John what were you thinking?". "Listen I know this is hard for you but I have to explain. Sandra has been kidnapped by the same guy that took the other girls and Shelley. We have until midnight New Year's Eve to find Sandra or he will kill her and I guess the baby as well. I am so mixed up, I told Sandra I would pay towards the upbringing of the child, but I wasn't going to play happy families" "What did she say?" "She accepted that but then when she got kidnapped, I feel such an eel, I have to find her." "John come here, I am not just your lover, I am your friend as well and your problems are my problems. I have missed you so much over the last few months since we split. When you came in the pub the other night

## The Poet And The Calling Card

I could feel butterfly's in my tummy. I love you John and I know deep down you love me too. I just have to wait until you have this out of your system." John could not believe how well Saron had taken the news.

John and Saron made passionate love. After the passion and love had been fulfilled, Saron had a little cry. "Hey what's the matter?" "Sorry John you have enough on your plate without me blubbering. You are going to think me silly but I always wanted children with you and I guess I wanted it to be perfect and have your first child. Now that chance has gone." "Saron, I never planned to have children and too be fair to Sandra I am sure she didn't. She has Rosie who she adores and was just getting her life back in order."

"Look get some sleep" "Are we going to see each other again?" "You have the pub now, so I suppose it will be when you get

## The Poet And The Calling Card

some time". "We don't make it easy do we John? What, with me and the pub, and you and your career?". Saron fell asleep on John's chest.

The following morning, with it being a Saturday, Saron had made John a full English breakfast. "What have you got planned today" "I am going into work. We have so little time to find Sandra." "Understand John" "Morning" "Morning Angelina, were you with Dave last night?" "That's for me to know and you to find out Saron" and she laughed, flicking her long dark hair as she wandered over to the kettle.

"Looks like the post has arrived" "Oh great, we should have that estimate for the conservatory today" said Saron. "You never said you were having a conservatory?" "Yes John, at the back. It's such a suntrap, we are increasing the dining capacity by about thirty percent." "Wow, well done." "Hey John, ther's a

## The Poet And The Calling Card

letter for you" "For me?" "Yes it's an Orange envelope, is it your birthday? and why they would send it here?"

John went cold knowing what the orange envelope meant to him. "Look ladies, I am going to nip home and get showered" "Ok John, nice to see you again" and Angelina emphasised the word "again". "I'll come to the car with you John." They walked across the car park, embraced and John said goodbye. Saron never said anything else she didn't want to pressurise him.

As John drove away he could see Saron in the rear view mirror waving, dressed in her fluffy white dressing gown. John thought how she looked like a movie star, she was incredibly good looking and her figure meant whatever she wore she looked a million dollars.

Once on the moor, John pulled over into a picnic area and opened the Orange

## The Poet And The Calling Card

envelope. This guy knew John's every move.

*"Dear John,*

*Well aren't you a clever boy then? You found your friend. What a nice Christmas present you have given to Jack Etchings!!*

*So now you have your little Princess, Miss Scooper, to think about. To be honest John, she cries that much I am tempted to garrotte her now, but I am a man of my word, as you surely know by now John.*

*Do you know you are so easy to follow about, very predictable? Your score so far, two you have saved, three you have let die. So you need this one to even the score John.*

*Time for another clue.*

## The Poet And The Calling Card

*Bread is made from this!!!*

*Happy hunting John. Oh and have a nice Christmas if we don't speak before. Tick Tock*

*The Poet."*

John showered and rang Donna. Donna sounded hung over. He went through what the Poet had said.

"I am on my way in Donna" "Look John, I will be in but it might be in a couple of hours. I'm not used to this partying" "No problem."

Gammon arrived at Bixton every detective was in, working on Sandra's case, John got everyone in the incident room.

"Ok everyone, thanks again for your efforts and for coming in this weekend to try and find Sandra. I had another letter from our killer this morning. As you are

## The Poet And The Calling Card

aware, the other day he had been to my house" Wally put his hand up. "No DNA, nothing, John this guy knows how we work."

"Well we have the following suspects.

Rinko Bolan the cleaner". Wally put his hand up again. "Another of your business cards was on Shelley Etchings. That means every victim has had your calling card John. I think this is personal". "Ok thanks, Wally."

"So, as I said, we have Rinko Bolan, an illegal immigrant who had access to Bixton Police station. The Orange envelopes, we have established, came from Poland. And he has a record of violence."

"Rachel Fiche, lesbian lover of Annabelle Leaf, one of the victims. This girl is a nasty piece of work, she has been convicted of violence and showed no

## The Poet And The Calling Card

emotion when she was interviewed with regard to Annabelle's demise."

"Reverend Matthew Spouncer, had connections with some of the victims through the church, he also found the first victim Mandy Nichol. Not a lot on this guy, other than he was a big friend of Stella Coles' biological father. Stella's friend, when interviewed by DI Smarty, said Stella had complained to her about him giving her the creeps and that he once tried to touch her inappropriately. Take that for what it is. The big connection is the church, which aligns with some of the victims".

"Gavin Strop, he was a nasty piece of work, he vowed to get even with me for putting him away. He was a violent man but having interviewed him, I think we can discount this suspect."

"Finally the ex-copper Lee Rune, there is a lot about this tosser I don't like. He is

## The Poet And The Calling Card

arrogant and confident my gut feeling is that either this is our man or it's Rachel Fiche, or maybe they work together? Let's see if we can find any connection with these two nasty pieces of work. He now lives in Ackbourne."

"We have to be aware that Sandra Scooper is under serious threat of death, if she is alive and I have no reason to believe she isn't, I received a clue this morning. It simply said "This makes bread!!". The previous clue said "Wet walls covered in slime". We have checked all the warehouses down by the canal but I would like a new team to check as well, just in case we have missed something."

"What about the old flour mill in Hittington Dale Sir?"

"Good thinking Milton, you and DI Lee go and search that. Ok team let's reconvene tomorrow. Thanks again for putting so

# The Poet And The Calling Card

much effort into finding your colleague, hopefully still alive."

John sat on his own in the incident room looking at the suspects and the small amount of evidence they had gathered.

"Sir, I've been looking everywhere for you, there was this Orange envelope on your car" "Get on the CCTV and shout me if you can see who put it there?" "Ok Sir." Gammon opened the envelope.

*"Hi John,*

*Me again, look I can't be doing with your DI Scooper much longer. So I am bringing forward the time you have to find her to Midnight Christmas Eve. She keeps saying she has tummy ache moaning cow.*

*So this is your final clue*

*My first is in Forest, but not in tree*

# The Poet And The Calling Card

*My second is in like, but not in hate*

*My third is in Oregon, but not in trail*

*My fourth is in weird, but not in straight*

*My fifth is in Emily but, not in Bishop*

*My sixth is in Rocket, but not in Ship*

*Tick Tock. The Poet*

*Oh, by the way, tell your Sergeant the CCTV doesn't work!!"*

Gammon rushed downstairs to Sergeant Yap. "What have you got?" "Sorry Sir, the CCTV is down" "Didn't you bloody know that? You are the bloody desk sergeant for goodness sake?". Just then DCI Fringe arrived looking the worse for wear. "Have you got a minute John?". She took him in the incident room. "What did I just walk into?" Gammon explained about the final letter and the CCTV. "Shit, I agree, he should have known, I'm sorry about this

# The Poet And The Calling Card

John. Get me a coffee let's see if together we can crack these bloody riddles."

They spent the next four hours working on the riddles, by this time Milton and Smarty were back. "Nothing in the old flour mill Ma'am" "Well we tried" "Did you check the floor for a basement?" asked John. "Yes Sir, we went through it with a fine tooth comb and with the dogs, there is nothing there."

"This is like looking for a needle in a haystack, he is going to kill her to spite me, I know he is" "John you don't know that" "What I do know Donna, is we don't have any idea where DI Scooper is being held and we have five days left."

"Where's Sergeant Milton, he is good with things like this?" "I'll get him John." "Carl take a look at this, what do you reckon?". Carl started going through the clues.

# The Poet And The Calling Card

"So she is being held somewhere damp at a guess. Bread? Well we have looked at the old flour mill and she isn't there. First is in Forest second is in Like, this isn't making something to do with bread?" "Look thanks Carl, but this is useless. I'm going home where I can think" Gammon got up and left.

He left the station and noticed he had a missed call from Steve Lineman. John called him back. "Hey mate you ok?" "Yeah, all good John. Bloody forgot to tell you, we are having a party at the house tonight, would love you to come" "What time mate?" "8.00pm onwards, stop the night here if you want" "You sure Jo doesn't mind?". "Of course not. Anyway Tracey, her sister, will be free if you get cold in the night old mate" "Behave yourself" "Right, I will see you tonight mate."

John got back to the cottage and Roger Glazeback met him as he was coming out

# The Poet And The Calling Card

of the milking parlour. "Hey John glad I caught you, seen a strange bloke hanging round your cottage. I know you had that break in the other week so I shouted and asked him what he wanted. He scarpered over the fields. I couldn't chase after him with having all these cows to milk." "Did you get a good look at him Roger?" "Not really, I was here at the entrance to the milking parlour and he was by your back door. He legged it before I could get a look at him." "Ok mate, well thanks for that."

John walked down to the limestone cottage and carefully opened the door. On the floor there was no envelope just one of his calling cards and a lock of hair. The card had blood smeared on it. John immediately phoned Wally in Forensics "If I come back Wally, can you check this out for me?" "Of course John."

John jumped back in his car and drove to Bixton station. "Back again Sir?"

# The Poet And The Calling Card

Gammon just nodded and headed straight to Forensics. "Grab a coffee John, it won't take me longer than half an hour to check for DNA and hopefully anything else". John went into the canteen and grabbed a coffee. Spot on half an hour, Wally was true to his word and he came with the results.

"The hair and the blood are DI Scoopers John." "Anything else Wally?" "Well it's difficult to say if it's from the crime scene but there are traces of pollen spores on the hair. It could be that she had this in her hair when she was kidnapped, but my feeling this has something to do with where she is being held John."

"Thanks Wally, I appreciate all you do mate." "John we are all as committed as you, we want to find Sandra." "I know that mate. Thanks again" and John left for the second time.

# The Poet And The Calling Card

He nipped back home got changed, still trying to work out the clues and the pollen on Sandra's hair. He can't be keeping her in a field this time of year, maybe she is in a greenhouse.

John felt frustrated, as drove up the long drive to Steve and Jo's beautiful home. He knocked on the front door it was 8.50pm. Tracey Rodgers answered the door. "Thought you had baled on us Mr Gammon" and she pecked John on the cheek Tracey had on a white dress, cut just above her knee. The dress had black side panels which complemented her blonde hair and brown eyes. "Come on in, the party is in full swing". John could see Bob and Cheryl, Tony Sherriff and Rita, they must have had a night off from the pub, Sheba Filey, Kev and Doreen, Joni and Carl, Carol Lestar. Jack Etchings was there, but he said Shelley wasn't quite up to it but she had insisted he came.

# The Poet And The Calling Card

They were soon dancing. One of John's favourites 'Stone Love' came on. Tracey grabbed his arm "Come on John". John was one these guys that took some persuading to get on the dance floor but once on there he didn't want to come off. "You can shake your booty Miss Rodgers" and he laughed. "You are not too bad yourself Mr Gammon".

Next up was 'Dancing Queen', ABBA. Tracey said she would fetch the drinks, she had no sooner left the dance floor, than Sheba had John dancing. Sheba whispered in John's ear "Are you staying over?". John was a bit taken back as Sheba had always played it cool. "Yeah Steve asked me to" "Well I am on the third bedroom down in the West wing, if you want drop by afterwards" and she smiled that gypsy look, with the sparkling teeth and then left, letting Tracey Rodgers take over. "She is very friendly Mr Gammon,

## The Poet And The Calling Card

one of the harem I guess?" "No just good friends Tracey, just good friends".

They came off the dance floor and stood with Steve and Jo. "Still got the moves Porky". John asked Steve which room he was in. "Whichever one you want why?" John told him what Sheba had said. "Go next door, second one down mate, nobody in that one tonight you jammy git." "You always fancied her didn't you Steve?" "You know I did. I chased her for a year and she always gave me the cold shoulder. Bloody Gammon strikes again". "What Steve?" asked Jo. "Oh nothing, me and John were talking about the old days" "Can you remember that far back?" "Ha Ha funny lady hey?" Jo smiled. "Another flippin' embarrassing moment averted Steve, you and your loud voice" said John.

"Any luck on Sandra mate?" "It's like looking for a needle in a haystack Steve, it really is. I think this guy is playing with us he seems to understand how we work".

# The Poet And The Calling Card

"Don't you have any suspects John?" "Yeah a few but for me only one strong one, a guy called Lee Rune an ex copper" "So why don't you arrest him?" "We don't have enough to hold him. Also if he is in custody then he can't give Sandra food and water if she is alive. Steve to be honest I think he will kill Sandra, he is twisted and he wants to get back at me." "Hey come on mate you are the best detective out there and if anybody can find Sandra it's you. Stop beating yourself up enjoy tonight if you relax a bit the clue may come to you."

"Thanks mate i can rely on you to see the good side" "Right what we drinking" "I'll have a large brandy mate" "Careful me old mucker, you will have to perform tonight" "Who said I would be going to Sheba's room anyway" "You will, you are a man aren't you?" and Steve laughed.

Jo had decked the house with four or five big Christmas tree's all nicely decorated,

## The Poet And The Calling Card

each tree having a different theme, there was a tree decorated in all gold, one in silver etc. The house was like something you see on Millionaires housewives, absolutely stunning.

After plenty of dancing, most of it with Tracey Rodgers, it was time to call it a night. Tracey didn't offer a night cap, so John was home and dry as he headed upstairs to his room, next door to Sheba's. He nipped in his room and freshened up and then went next door to Sheba's. As he entered her room it was all in darkness. "Sheba, Sheba?" No answer, he fumbled around trying to find the light switch. Eventually he found it and flicked it on. The room was empty, on the bed John could see a stuffed sheep and a note.

"Hi John, you missed your chance, so I have left you my sheep Dillon, to sleep with. Sweet dreams Mr Gammon."

# The Poet And The Calling Card

Bugger Sheba had played him again. John saw the funny side, so he took the note and Dillon back to his room. It was perhaps a good job Sheba had played him, the Brandy was taking a big effect and soon he was fast asleep.

The following morning John woke it was almost 9.00am, he could smell bacon cooking, so he showered and changed making his way down to the kitchen. Jo and Tracey were cooking a full English breakfast. There was John, Tracey, Jo, Steve, Carol Lestar, Bob and Cheryl. No sign of Sheba. Steve sat next to John and winked. "What you winking at?" In a soft voice, which was hard for Steve to do, he said "You know, last night, was it good?" John thought he would play the game by not saying.

Steve laughed "So you had a good night with the stuffed sheep then?" "How the hell did you know Lineman?" "Well I know Sheba arrived with one and when

## The Poet And The Calling Card

she asked if she could move rooms, I carried her case to the East wing and she said she was leaving the stuffed sheep for the next occupant. "What? and you never told me you git." Steve by now was laughing uncontrollably. "What's so funny Steve?" "Nothing Carol just a private joke with John". They carried on with the breakfast. "So where is Sheba?" "She left at 6.30pm and I had to move the car to let her out, she said she couldn't stop for breakfast as she had family up from Suffolk". "You were totally had detective" "Bollocks, some mate you are" and John laughed.

"Right listen mate, I need to get into work, every hour wasted is an hour Sandra has left to live" "Understand mate, good luck and thanks for coming". John thanked Jo and said his goodbyes to everyone.

Arriving at Bixton, it was a cold morning and the heating had failed at the station, everyone was walking round with their

# The Poet And The Calling Card

coats on. "Anything new on Scooper Sergeant Yap?" "Nothing Sir, oh there was an Orange envelope addressed to you, it was on my car this morning". Yap handed it over to John. John grabbed a coffee, he could see the rest of the team were busy in the incident room. Gammon thought, what a good team he had, they had given their weekend up to try and find Sandra. He grabbed a hot coffee, his office windows still had the morning frost on them, with no heating it was hellishly cold in his office.

John opened the Orange envelope.

*Dear John,*

*I have to say I thought with the clue's I gave you, that you would have found Scooper by now. I have to report, she is not looking good as the clock ticks. I have cut down on the bread I give her, I mean when she dies, it's a waste to die on*

## The Poet And The Calling Card

*a full stomach"* and he had drawn a smiley face.

*I have been thinking about what I will do if you don't get to Scooper in time. Should I grab another one to test you or wait a while. Let's face it John, you haven't got a clue who I am and I find that really funny. The great John Gammon looks like losing a colleague. I know when she dies the police will be throwing every resource at finding me. I think to myself sometimes, do I just stop feeding her now with three days to go? and jump on a plane to somewhere nice for the winter? then come back and torment you again or do I have one last hurrah.*

*You see John, I don't like killing, it's not something that is nice but it is necessary, all will be revealed as to the reasons why in good time.*

# The Poet And The Calling Card

*I wish you luck (don't really mean that) just remember Tick Tock John.*

*The Poet."*

Gammon went straight down to the Incident room to share the letter from the killer with everyone.

"Come on team, this has to be Rune, everything fits. He is an ex copper, he knows how we work. He has a massive grudge against me. Put the clues on the board again, let's all study them and see if we can come up with something".

Gammon wrote them out again and they all took notes. Suddenly John had a Eureka moment "Llook at the words and the first letter of each word then look down".

Forest

Like

# The Poet And The Calling Card

Oregon

Weird

Emily

Rocket

"What do you all see team? Inspector Lee?" "Flower" "Correct. He is playing with us, DI Scooper had pollen in her hair from the lock of hair he sent us. So I think he is telling us she is somewhere where there will be flowers. Come on thinking head on time".

"Blimey John there are three flower shops in Bixton, two in Ackbourne then there is one in Swinster, one in Pritwich and four in Micklock." "Right split up, call the owners, we want all the shops looking at. Also check outbuildings and cellars, she must be at one of these."

# The Poet And The Calling Card

With great haste they all set off. John shouted "Report back here in the morning unless we find something. Also take two dog teams, they may pick up a scent from Scooper's lock of hair."

The whole team set off to check all the shops out. Gammon and Milton did the villages, first Pritwich, eventually getting the owner out, with it being Sunday. Nothing found. Then they went to Swinster to Fairies and Flowers Shop owned by a Miss Kimberley Drake. She also wasn't too happy, they checked the shop out but nothing. There was no cellar but there was a red bricked out building. "What's in there Miss Drake?" "I don't know, never been in, I only rent the shop". "Come on Carl". The door to the outbuilding had a big pad lock on it. After considerable effort they forced entry. It was pitch black, Kimberley Drake came back with a small torch she kept in her car.

# The Poet And The Calling Card

Gammon shone it, he could see at the back of the room an outline of a figure sat down. He shouted, "Sandra, Sandra?". No answer they walked over mindful that the killer also set up traps, like he did with Stella Coles.

Finally Milton shone the torch at the figure, it was mannequin sat on a chair. "Shit I thought we had found her Sir" "So did I Carl". There was nothing else in the outbuilding so they left the shop.

The other teams were reporting back, nobody had found anything.

"Looks like another wild goose chase Sir?" "Worth a try Carl, she has to be round here somewhere".

It was 6.20pm when DI Smarty, who was at the last shop identified to look at, called Gammon. "Sorry John, nothing." "Well thanks for giving up your time Dave. We might as well call it a day Carl." said John.

## The Poet And The Calling Card

"Do you fancy a pint?" Do you know Carl, I could murder one, where do you want to go?" "I went to the Tow'd Man the other night, they had a Christmas beer on called Santa Baby, really nice". "That will do for me Carl".

They set off for the Tow'd man, the whole of the valley was awash with fresh snow. Branches of the trees were laden with snow. It was so beautiful John thought. Carl had gone off first, so John was following when his phone rang. "Mr Gammon? Lady Hasford, Sandra's Mum" "Oh hello". "I am worried John, do you have anything new?" "I am so sorry Lady Hasford the team have worked all over the weekend, we thought we had a lead but it went cold". "He is going to kill my daughter isn't he Mr Gammon?" "I don't know that, Sandra is very resourceful Lady Hasford, I am still optimistic we will find her?". John could feel a lump come in

## The Poet And The Calling Card

his throat deep down he knew Sandra's time maybe up.

He finally arrived at the Tow'd Man, Carl had ordered two pints of Santa baby. "What strength is it Carl?" "7.4% Sir" "John, call me John" "Sorry John its habit". The Aussie was behind the bar, no sign of Saron or Angelina. "Shall we sit in the window Carl?" "Can I ask you something John?" "Of course mate what is it?" "It's Joni, we are so on and off I don't seem to be able to do right for doing wrong. After Beth I think I jumped in too soon". "Look Carl the man that understands how women work, hasn't been born mate. They are an enigma to me mate, like every other man in the world. All I will say is, she is a terrific girl but you have to decide if she is the girl for you Carl."

Angelina appeared, "Evening lads, I have to say you two look the life and soul of the party. What's up?" "Still no joy trying to

## The Poet And The Calling Card

find Sandra" "I am sure you will crack it" "We only have two days left Angelina" "I thought the deadline was New Year's Eve?" "He brought it forward to midnight Christmas Eve" "The evil bastard John, excuse my French. What possess these evil people?"

"I don't know but I feel he is taunting me and Sandra is caught up in it, if we don't find her in time I will never forgive myself." "Come on, you'll find her. let me get you both a drink." Angelina came back with two large brandies "Get those down you, they will make you feel better" and she disappeared back to the bar. By 10.30pm both Carl and John had had enough, so they went on their way.

It was now Christmas Eve morning and John left for Bixton station, he decided to drive on the back roads to try and clear his mind. As John drove through Cowdale it suddenly hit him. For many years cut flowers, sold from Chatsworth, had been

# The Poet And The Calling Card

stored in Cowdale at building there. As a little boy he had known it as Hermits Retreat. Legend had it that for many years a Hermit lived there but he wasn't sure if that was actually true. What he did know was, it was worth a look.

Gammon parked his car on Up The Steps Maggie's car park and followed the steps down into the Dale. There was only one set of footprints going both ways along the Dale. Gammon finally arrived at the large stone building, he had noticed the track led to the Hermits Retreat, the returning footprints in the snow were new, so whoever had been here had not long left. Gammon walked to the building which was heavily padlocked with a big lock and a chain, the type bikers put round their motorbike wheels. With nothing to cut it off with, Gammon went round the side of the building. The windows were covered in cobwebs and you could smell the damp with it being next to the river.

## The Poet And The Calling Card

Gammon decided to put a window through and climb in. Once through the window, he wasn't ready for what was going to greet him. In the corner was Sandra, she was covered in blood like she had been beaten but she appeared to be wired to some contraption. Gammon pulled out his phone. Although the signal was poor, he got through to Sergeant Yap and told him to send a bomb disposal unit and an ambulance.

Gammon daren't touch Sandra for fear of blowing the device. She seemed to be out of it. Maybe that was a good thing with what had to be done. Fifteen minutes passed, when all hell broke loose, they caved in the door and ordered Gammon outside while they attended to the device wired to Sandra. Gammon was forced back over twenty yards to behind the Police line. They bomb squad took almost two hours to release Sandra and she was immediately taken away in an Ambulance.

# The Poet And The Calling Card

Gammon followed informing DCI Donna Fringe of the situation. "Well done John, I hope she is ok?" "I will let you know Donna".

Another four hours passed, Sandra was in intensive care. They brought her up to a private room but she was in a coma. "Are you the husband?" a doctor asked. "No, I am a colleague" "Oh do you have a contact for her family?". John remembered her mother had phoned him, so he called her and told her the situation.

Lady Hasford arrived and the doctor took her into a side room. She explained to the doctor about the baby and that John was the father, so he was allowed into the doctor's office.

"I am afraid Sandra is very, very poorly, she has lost her baby and I have to be honest with you and say you may lose Sandra. She was badly beaten and kicked, we believe one kick to her stomach

## The Poet And The Calling Card

actually killed the baby and that is one of the reason she is so ill."

"I would suggest you go home and we will call if there is any change but this could take months, not weeks before we know if she will survive and if she does if there will be lasting damage."

John comforted Lady Hasford. "Are you ok to drive Lady Hasford?" "Yes, I will be fine Mr Gammon. I am sorry, I didn't say thank you for finding my Sandra".

Gammon drove home, it was Christmas Eve but his whole body ached with fear that not only had he lost his baby but there was every likely hood he would lose Sandra. There was no Annie Tanney this time to help, he thought.

Once back at the cottage lay on the mat was a dreaded Orange envelope.

# The Poet And The Calling Card

*Dear John,*

*It is time I revealed myself and the reason for all this. Before I do, although I hate you with a passion, I didn't know DI Scooper was pregnant and for that I am sorry.*

*Cast your mind back to the day I told you about Rune, we all served together and you being mister right and proper and the rising star in the force did nothing wrong.*

*Well you wrecked Rune's life when you reported him. What you didn't know was I was on the take, I knew Rune would not shop me and it deflected any suspicion away from me. We all used to laugh at you and your whiter than white persona.*

*With Rune gone, some of the other guys knew I was involved with Rune, I was ostracised you got promotion and moved on. I eventually decided a move would be*

# The Poet And The Calling Card

*the best option, they were closing in on me. I ended up in Rotherham in Yorkshire.*

> *I decided one day after I was pensioned off when that bloody skank shot me that I would get the great John Gammon. I lay in that hospital bed knowing my time in the force was over. One day I read an article on the new rising star, John bloody Gammon, and it really pissed me off so I hatched a plan.*

*Everything you have seen was a set up. I married that stupid woman, it was somewhere to live while I hatched my revenge all part of the bigger plan. Then her stupid daughter caught me out, she said she wouldn't say anything but I could not take that chance until I had done all the deeds. I found that place near Ardwalk and I wired her up, it was either going to be you if you guessed the poems or some inquisitive walker, but at*

## The Poet And The Calling Card

*least it would not be me that killed her, I just wired her up.*

*The first one I did was designed to lead you to the Church, as were some of the others. I knew you would pick up on Matthew Spouncer and I knew you would clock the picture of him on the mantelpiece. What a prat I made of the great John Gammon.*

*The real fun was taking your friend Shelley Etchings and watching you being powerless when your friend was asking if you would find her.*

*DI Scooper, funnily enough I met her when she was a PC, she won't remember but I remembered her and when I called for a drink in Swinster, I overheard a woman talking about you and Scooper being an item. Well I could not resist the opportunity to give you more anguish.*

# The Poet And The Calling Card

*By the way, did you like the John Gammon cards? I knew you would look at the cleaner Mr Rinko Bolan. I checked his record and it wasn't good so he was an ideal smoke screen.*

*Then poor old Rune, the fall guy again, I was hoping you would charge him once Scooper was dead, because I was then going to send an open letter to a national newspaper outlining why it wasn't him, but you spoiled that today Gammon.*

*Anyway you will never find me and I will be back. You will be my victim seven, then you can know what they went through to shame you, big shot. I will sign off and wish you a Happy Christmas. Keep looking over your shoulder Super Cop, we aren't finished yet.*

*Glyn Grant (Whisky) you now know me as the Poet."*

# The Poet And The Calling Card

John sat back absolutely flabbergasted, he rung Donna and told her. They put an arrest warrant out for Glyn Grant but deep down John knew this guy was cute he knew his way around.

With Sandra in a coma, the baby lost, all these murders and upset, just because he was hated by Whisky left John feeling down.

Would Sandra pull through? Would this maniac show himself again, only this time John be the victim? Questions he didn't know the answers to.

To be continued
................................

# The Poet And The Calling Card

The Following books are from the author C J Galtrey.

## The John Gammon Peak District Detective
### Series One

**Book One:** Things Will Never Be The Same Again.

**Book Two:** Sad Man.

**Book Three:** Joy Follows Sorrow.

**Book Four:** Never Cry On A Bluebell.

**Book Five:** Annie Tanney.

### Series Two

**Book One:** The Poet and The Calling Card

**Book Two:** Why

The following books are not John Gammon books but also from the author C J Galtrey

Looking for Shona: An historical love story with time travel.

Got to keep Running: A successful businesswomen's fight to stay alive who does she trust?

# The Poet And The Calling Card

Please visit my website or Facebook page for new books and updates.

www.colingaltrey.co.uk

I hope you are enjoying all my books. All the books are in paperback or Kindle format and the first book "Things Will Never Be The Same Again" is due for release on audio the first week of December 2016 closely followed by all my books that are on general release.

You can now take John Gammon with you in the car or relax at home and listen to the characters come to life in the beautiful Peak District of Derbyshire.

C J Galtrey

Made in the USA
Columbia, SC
14 July 2017